APOSTATE PRIEST

Wanda Ann Thomas

CHAPTER 1

Jerusalem 30 BC

E ight years had elapsed since James Onias walked the immaculate streets of Jerusalem. The white-walled sepulcher of the Temple loomed ahead. The stink of the burnt offering assaulted his nose. Worshipers fresh from ritual baths swarmed out of gates presided over by Temple guardsmen armed with clubs.

Hate for his birthplace throbbed to life like an awakened toothache.

He recognized most of the men, but they had yet to identify him—his Roman garb and smooth-shaven face and severe Julian-style haircut fooled others, but he found it impossible to forget he was an apostate priest of Israel. If he hadn't forsaken his birthright, he would be Chief Doorkeeper.

James put his head down and walked on.

He had no one to blame but himself. He ought to have remained in Rome and left this door of his life closed. The betrayal by his father. The war years when he'd spied for Herod. The brief, unhappy marriage to Kitra.

But no.

King Herod, rot him, had held out a gem too tempting

to reject.

The prize–the title of master builder.

James almost wished the powerful quake that had rocked Jerusalem the previous year had tumbled every stone and swallowed the city. Then Herod might not be using the wreck and ruin as an opportunity to rebuild Jerusalem to his liking. The invitation from the king mentioned aqueducts, amphitheater, gymnasium, a Roman-style bath, hippodrome, palace-fortresses, and a grand vision for rebuilding the Temple.

Many would scoff at the notion of the Hellenization of Jerusalem. But anyone unfortunate enough to stand in the path of the warrior-soldier who made himself king, quickly learned the foolishness of underestimating Herod.

James's problem was that he lusted to be named Herod's master builder.

He veered left down a narrow alley, relieved to put the Temple at his back.

The sound of sandals slapping on stone greeted him, and a red-headed young man knocked him to the ground.

"Watch where you are going!" he growled, rubbing his bloody elbow.

Spouting apologies, the young man helped James to his feet.

He brushed the dirt from his expensive tunic. "Imbecile! Why the infernal hurry?"

An ecstatic urgency lit the young man's face. "I didn't want to miss the execution."

James examined the lad more closely. He recognized the palace slave and fellow spy. "Niv?"

The slave's pudgy face had thinned, his freckles had almost completely faded, and he had doubled in height.

Niv sobered. "James Onias. You haven't heard the news about Elizabeth Boethus?"

Dread knotted his gut. Libi was supposed to be residing safely in Egypt. "Elizabeth is in Jerusalem?"

"They are about to execute her." Niv jogged away.

Abject terror grabbed James by the spine. Cursing the sluggishness of his thirty-two-year-old legs as he struggled to catch up, he followed Niv out of the alley. "Execution? What nonsense is this?"

Niv weaved around donkey carts and food vendors and pedestrian. "She was caught in adultery."

James did not believe it for a moment. Not his Libi. She was all that was pure and good. "Who are her accusers?

"The trial and judgment happened lightning quick. That is all I know."

Lies and murderous intent were responsible. That was the only thing that made even remote sense.

They sprinted through the double-arched gate, scattering a goat herd. "They have not started yet," Niv said, amid the bleating of the goats and the shouts of the fist-waving goat herder.

A crowd seethed at the edge of a rocky precipice.

James veered toward a group of bronzed, muscled stonecutters making repairs to the city wall. Digging out gold coins from the cloth bag tied to his belt, he snatched a hammer from a dirt-covered hand and tossed the coins at the shocked man. "For your trouble," he yelled over his shoulder, and raced away.

Niv slowed to allow James to catch up. "What are you doing?"

"If they insist on executing Libi, they will have to kill me first." James tested the weight of the hammer. "I will not make it easy for them."

"Holy hellfire!"

"Exactly," James muttered and plunged into the outer ring of the mob. He barely avoided knocking down women and children, but felt no such constraint shoving his way past men of low rank.

He burst into the inner circle of Sadducees, Pharisees, and priests just as a young man flopped face-first onto the ground at the removal of the rope around his neck.

A deafening roar filled James's ears. His sole focus was Elizabeth.

Tears stained her ivory cheeks and dirt soiled her simple white sleeping gown. A blind leper could not have looked more isolated and alone.

Hot coals burned in a nearby iron brazier holding a steaming cauldron of melted lead and tin. A blank-faced executioner stood at the ready with the sturdy cord wrapped in a soft cloth. It would be used to force Libi's mouth open as the molten liquid was poured down her throat. A ghastly penalty reserved for the daughters of priests guilty of adultery.

Horror and rage roiled James's innards. "Elizabeth," he croaked.

Terror shone in her black eyes. "James!" She rushed into his arms and buried her face in his chest. "Thank the Lord."

He tucked her under his arm.

The crowd erupted in curses and protests.

He pulled her closer, hefted the hammer, and narrowed his eyes at those eager to witness her death. "Go home. Today's entertainment is finished."

Elizabeth clawed at his tunic. "I am innocent. You believe me?"

His heart broke. "Absolutely, and to my dying breath.

Which hopefully comes after we both live to be as old as Moses."

"How can you jest?"

James's eyes shifted to Saul Boethus, Elizabeth's supposedly aggrieved husband, stepping over the body of the dead man.

Tall and lean, with blunt-cut black hair, Saul was known as the Egyptian. And for good reason, as he looked more like Cleopatra than a Jew, with his sleek goatee and eyes lined with black kohl. Dabs of red ocher colored his cheeks.

But that was not why James could not stand the sight of the man. In their youth, James and Saul had lived in Rome as apprentices to the city's finest master builders. They had been rivals from the start, with Saul gaining the upper hand in Egypt as a rising star in Cleopatra's court. The queen's recent defeat at Actinium and subsequent suicide must be responsible for Saul's presence in Jerusalem.

The Egyptian looked down his long nose at James. "Stand aside, James Onias."

Elizabeth stiffened. "Why are you doing this?"

"I caught my brother-in-law and the adulteress in the act of adultery."

"It is not true," Elizabeth spit back.

Temple guardsmen and high-ranking priests advanced on them.

James waved the hammer threateningly. Two faces stood out, Benjamin and Banna, stringy-haired twins who had grown up next door to James. But he forgot about them when the ranks of priests parted, revealing Elizabeth's brother, Andrew.

Bitterness and meanness tainted his cousin's donkey

face. "There were witnesses."

"They lied," Elizabeth said, her tone pleading. "Why will you not believe me?"

Andrew's features did not soften. "Accept your fate. Step forward and die with dignity."

"Let's go." James backed away, drawing Elizabeth with him. "There is no justice to be had here."

"What do you think you are doing?" Andrew demanded.

James did not have a plan other than to get Elizabeth to safety. Turning, he was shocked to find Niv in the company of the stonecutters. The slave's smile was broad. "They said they were friends of yours."

James had spent the happiest years of his life living and working among Jerusalem's stonecutters. He tossed the hammer to the rightful owner, a rugged fellow from Galilee whose name escaped him. "I'd be grateful if you slow down anyone who tries to follow us."

The fellow grinned. Like many Galileans, he delighted in opposing Jerusalem's religious elite, who tended to look down their noses at the less educated countrymen. "If the mood strikes you, come wield a hammer at the work site."

"I might take you up on that," James called as he fled with Elizabeth.

The angry shouts directed at them and the stonecutters slowly dimmed.

Disaster was averted for now, but it would take a miracle to untangle the mess.

Or a grand favor, courtesy of King Herod.

CHAPTER 2

Elizabeth Onias Boethus paced the cramped windowless chamber. A mere half hour removed from a horrible fate, her stomach sickened at her narrow escape. James Onias's palatial ancestral home was the last place in the world she would choose to take refuge. At the moment, it represented her only safety.

An unhinged laugh escaped her lips. The likelihood of a priest's daughter convicted of adultery escaping Jerusalem alive was non-existent.

Perched on the edge of a massive desk, James Onias raised an eyebrow. His sapphire-blue tunic was the only spot of color in the gray surroundings.

She clapped her hand to her mouth and paced faster. If there was any mercy in the world, she would wake to find all of this simply a nightmare.

James shifted his weight and crossed his arms over his wide chest. "The doors and windows are barred. And Niv should return any moment with the Roman guards."

"You seem very sure King Herod will comply with the request," she answered, annoyed at his unnatural calm.

He shrugged. "He will not allow an angry mob to kill his master builder."

She halted and planted her fists on her hips. "Jerusalem is not Rome or Egypt. Sin and sinners cannot be pushed under a rug."

"What sin? You are innocent."

She exhaled a shaky breath. "Bless you for believing me."

"I will not allow them to kill you."

The past eight years had seen James put on a surprising amount of bulk consisting mostly of muscle. Without his beard, the purple braided scar on his right cheek stood out vividly. Coupled with his short-clipped hair, it made him an imposing figure. There was a certain beauty to his darkness.

She blushed at the direction of her thoughts. "Where do we go from here?"

Preoccupied in thought, James thumbed the scar. "How long have you and your husband been in Jerusalem? And why does he want you dead?"

She swallowed. Answering the first question was safe.

"Saul had enjoyed great favor with Cleopatra and Antony. After the queen's defeat and death, the construction projects ground to a halt with no new work coming in. We arrived a few days ago, after a hasty journey upon learning King Herod was searching for a master builder."

James's brow furrowed. "Has Saul won favor with the king?"

"Not that I know of. But Saul does not confide in me."

"Has the marriage been difficult on you?" he asked, his expression softening.

What could she safely say about the marriage and her life in Egypt?

"Not difficult. But very different from my life in Jerusalem."

"Saul always was a strange fellow."

"And you and Kitra?" she asked.

"The marriage did not last long." He looked away and exhaled heavily. "I was a horrible husband."

Kitra was a flirtatious seductress. No one who knew her would be surprised if she was guilty of adultery. Elizabeth bit her lip at the unkind thought. "I heard she remarried a Nabatean prince."

"They say the prince has kicked her out."

"I wish there was not so much sadness in the world."

James pushed away from the desk and joined her, coming too close for comfort.

"Do not feel bad for Kitra. She will not be down for long. She is a fighter and a survivor."

Was that fondness and respect in his voice? Elizabeth set aside her curiosity.

"The morning started out peacefully," she explained. "Saul had rented a large, well-appointed home from a widow in the upper city. I had just finished bathing and was dressing in a clean tunic, when my drunken brother-in-law Jonah forced his way into my room. Before I had time to recover from my surprise, he stripped away his tunic, pushed me onto the bed, and..."

Recalling the incident iced her insides. Her revulsion and fear at his groping hands sliding over her. Her crying for him to stop. Her desperate struggle to escape.

James tenderly brushed at the tears streaming down her face. But there was nothing gentle about his voice. "If this Jonah fellow was not dead, I would strangle the cretin myself."

His ferocity on her behalf was strangely comforting.

She clasped her shaking hands together. "Saul and my sister-in-law Phaedra entered the bedchamber and spewed vile recriminations. I pleaded with them to believe I was innocent. Jonah claimed they had caught us in a love spat in what was a short, but torrid affair. I vehemently denied it. But his lies did not stop there. I could not have been more shocked or aghast when Jonah produced love letters written in my hand."

"Forgeries," James said, then swore foully. "Someone went to a lot of trouble to make you look guilty."

"That makes sense. Jonah never looked me in the eye once during the hurried trial and his mumbled confession. I was not allowed to testify, and no one stepped forward in my defense. Not even my own brother."

"Andrew is a pious—"

"Be kind," she chided. "He never got over his bitterness about our father's long-term affair with the Samaritan woman. It is natural he would believe I was guilty of the same sin as my father."

"Visiting the iniquities of the fathers on the children," James said in a disgusted tone.

She winced. Andrew had thrown those very words at her. "My brother is miserable. He hates his wife."

"Our fathers did not do well by us."

Her father and James's father had made the mistake of siding with Herod's enemies in the last war. The cost of making peace with King Herod was marriages of alliance for James, Andrew, and Elizabeth. James had married Herod's niece Kitra. Andrew became husband to Herod's lame niece. And Elizabeth was shipped off to Egypt to wed the master builder Saul.

The time for blame was past. Both of their fathers were dead and buried. She squeezed James's hand. "Let them rest in peace."

His black eyes pierced hers. "Hardly a day passes when

I do not regret refusing to marry you all those years ago."

She released his hands as though singed. "Stop! I am your stepmother. Talk of that kind is inappropriate."

Desperate to keep his affair with the Samaritan woman a secret, her father had given her in marriage to his fifty-three-year-old cousin Simeon Onias. James's father had been perpetually hateful and unkind as he schemed and plotted to win the position of High Priest of Israel. The marriage had lasted only six months. But each day had been pure misery. And though eighteen years had passed since Simeon Onias had divorced her and sent her home, she never failed to celebrate the banner day.

James captured her by the elbows. "Tell me you do not remember the kisses we shared in your father's garden."

She shook free and retreated. How many nights had she woken from dreams in a fevered sweat? Dreams that went much further than impassioned kisses.

"That was wrong." The sharp rebuke was aimed at herself, as well as James. "Do not speak to me of it again."

James followed her. "The marriage to my father was never consummated, was it?"

She bumped up against the desk, the very desk where Simeon Onias had once presided, insulting and scolding and belittling her and James and his household slaves. "Where did you hear that?"

"From you." Looming over her, James simmered with anger.

"I never—"

"I heard you with my own ears call him a withered up she-goat," James contended. "His manhood was dried up and useless when you married, wasn't it? His last wife confirmed my suspicion. Tell me I am wrong."

Her face heated. All he said was true. "What does it

matter?"

"I loved you." He caged her against the desk. "We could have married."

She covered her face. "Why do you have to ruin everything? I do not want to fight. I have not even had time to thank you for fulfilling your promise to find a cure for my...ailment."

"You stopped bleeding?" The aggression on his face gave way to a rare smile. "Which potion worked? Let me guess. The cure from the Ethiopian midwife."

It was impossible not to be embarrassed. The start of her monthly flow of blood that had marked her passage into womanhood had never completely ceased, rendering her as *zavah*—ritually unclean. Though she'd had no correspondence with James these last eight years, she would intermittently receive packages of medicine and accompanying detailed instructions for use and concocting of the cures. One finally showed promise.

"The bitter taste almost discouraged me, but within a few days the cramps lessoned and after a few weeks the —" her face grew hotter "—the bleeding stopped."

"I cannot tell you how happy this news makes me." He touched her sleeve. "I can secure more of the herbs for you if you are unable to obtain them."

The simple gesture of his touch meant more to her than he could know. Her *zavah* condition had been a heavy burden to bear when she resided in Jerusalem. People avoided her or whispered behind her back. Far worse, she was isolated in her own home, as her brothers and father were Temple priests and officers who must maintain ritual purity. But James had never viewed her as tainted or treated her differently.

"Saul has seen to that. But please accept my fondest

gratitude." She patted his hand. Exhaustion crept into her bones. "I had my heart set on visiting the Temple after all the purity rituals were attended to, but now...."

"You will worship at the Temple again," James promised.

She laughed weakly. "I will do well to escape Jerusalem alive."

James's intense black eyes locked on her. "You are innocent. We will prove it."

"But how?" She wanted to believe him.

A knock sounded at the door.

"Master," a slave called out. "Niv has returned with a large contingent of guards."

"Herod sending help is a good sign," James said, and rushed to the door. "You should be safe enough while I pay a visit to the king." He departed without giving her a chance to reply.

She rubbed her chilled arms.

James Onias and King Herod were her champions.

The angels help her.

CHAPTER 3

A half hour after his arrival at the Hasmonean Palace, James was escorted into King Herod's private quarters. There was nothing private or humble about the high-ceilinged, marble-columned reception chamber. Arrangements of over-sized plush couches and chairs accommodated the extended royal family and palace guests. The king's young nieces and nephews, the liveliest ones, were playing a dice game. Off to one corner, Herod's four young children romped freely under the indulgent eyes of the king's beautiful wife, Mariamne.

Members of the royal court huddled in small groups, divided into opposing factions. Military, domestic, and religious advisers, each hoping to gain the upper hand in the constant battle to earn the king's favor. The chamber could have easily accommodated another hundred people.

At the center of the crowd, King Herod presided from a small dais, seated on a throne-like chair. The newly appointed High Priest Joshua ben Fabus, a mousy looking man, occupied one of the modest chairs flanking the king.

Judging from their fierce demeanors and stiff postures, the Egyptian Saul and his sister Phaedra were haranguing the king and Fabus, likely to take immediate action against Elizabeth. Elizabeth's brother Andrew was absent. A good sign. At least, James hoped it was a good sign.

Teeth painfully clenched, he charged ahead.

The Temple priests and guardsmen led by the twin priests Benjamin and Banna blocked his path.

Banna's stringy hair hung in eyes filled with sorrow. "Will you never stop shaming your family and your brethren?"

James's loathing and disgust for Temple officers and their holier-than-thou attitudes roared to life. He shoved Banna aside. "Shame on you for believing lies spread by Saul Boethus."

James halted in front of Saul.

The Egyptian's lips pursed, accentuating the v shape of his goatee. "Haven't you caused enough trouble for one day?"

James enjoyed a grin at Saul's expense. "You were not expecting someone to step forward to deliver Elizabeth from your treachery, were you?"

Saul's kohl-rimmed eyes were filled with calculation, rather than the anger or betrayal to be expected of a man who has caught his wife in bed with another man. "First you abduct my wife. Now you make false accusations."

Saul's older sister Phaedra eyed James as if he was a loathsome sea creature. She also dressed and styled her hair and makeup in Egyptian fashion. "While you bleat over Elizabeth's innocence the adulteress is likely washing away the evidence of my husband's seed."

An uproar arose.

Blushing crimson, High Priest Joshua ben Fabus called

for calm.

"Your husband attacked Elizabeth." Glaring at Phaedra, James nearly choked on his outrage.

King Herod raised his hand, signaling for silence. A robust and powerful man of forty-five, Herod would have been intimidating even without being king. As absolute sovereign, he was doubly formidable and deadly.

James fisted his hands and stepped boldly to the dais.

"You will never have my services as master builder if this conniving pair are allowed to murder Elizabeth Onias."

King Herod stared at him for many long tense moments, then roared with laughter.

"James, I see you have not lost any of your sour charm. Come and sit. I am anxious to hear about the small temple you constructed in Herculaneum."

James's tongue was stuck to the roof of his desert-dry mouth. Tempted to keep railing on Elizabeth's behalf, he climbed the stairs of the small stage.

"All of Rome is saying it is the prettiest temple in the land," Herod said enthusiastically.

Phaedra whispered in her brother's ear.

The Egyptian made a loud throat-clearing noise. "What of our grievances? Are we—"

"Leave us," Herod ordered icily.

Saul wisely departed with his unhappy sister in tow. Benjamin and Banna and the other priests skulked away as well. But there would surely be plenty of private grumbling over Herod's handling of the matter.

Saul turned back and speared James with a defiant look. *You haven't won yet*, his eyes said.

James agreed. King Herod might turn on him yet. And it was highly doubtful High Priest Fabus would take a woman's word—Elizabeth's—over Saul's. Fabus would no doubt cherish lording it over James in retribution for his apostate ways.

Though it galled, James acknowledged High Priest Fabus with a bow of the head, fully prepared to grovel at the priest's feet if that was what was required to save Elizabeth from Saul's lies.

A flick of Herod's finger sent the High Priest rushing away.

James should not chuckle, but the poison of self-righteous men like Fabus, who delighted in throwing stones at *sinners* as they denied their own wickedness, brought out the worst in him. "They hate your guts."

Herod's weary grunt spoke volumes.

"Sit." He pointed to the chair abandoned by Fabus.

Settling on the still-warm seat, James was keenly aware of the watchful stares from all corners of the reception hall. The assembly did not care two figs about James's plight. No, gauging the king's every shift of mood was essential for surviving and thriving in this, or any, royal court.

James swallowed. Herod was an unpredictable man in the best of times. With *only* Elizabeth's life hanging in the balance, he groped for the best approach to take.

"I am interested in hearing of your impressions of Emperor Octavian." The king leaned on the arm of the throne.

Eight years ago James had served as a spy for Herod. Was this a test? To Herod's way of thinking, if he engaged James to be his master builder, he would also be acquiring a trusted spy.

James smiled with the knowledge of the distinct edge this gave him over the Egyptian. "I was fortunate enough to attend several state banquets. Do not cut off my head for saying so, but I was quite impressed with the man."

"He is quite young to be leading an empire."

"Thirty-three is young," James agreed. "But underestimating Octavian would be a mistake. Antony and Cleopatra did, and you know how that ended."

His eyes darkening, Herod gnawed on his thumb for a moment.

"I had no choice but to side with Antony. His armies could have crushed me as easily as a bug underfoot. What else could I do?"

James considered. Herod's nervousness made sense.

"I hear Octavian is moving quickly to consolidate his power."

Herod reached inside his robe and produced an official-looking document.

"I received a notification advising me to get my affairs in order and to be prepared to depart at a moment's notice for Rhodes to present my case to Octavian."

James's concern for Herod's welfare was selfish. "Octavian will not find a more loyal friend to Rome than you."

"I agree." Herod's mouth was a grim slash. "But my enemies are hoping Octavian sends me to the grave. My body will not have time to grow cold before my enemies grab the throne for themselves."

Countless Israelites wished Herod ill. Born of an Idumean father and Nabatean mother, he was not considered a true Jew. They would never forgive him for making himself king.

"Who poses the most danger?"

"My wife, mother-in-law, and John Hyrcanus. Their royal blood will appeal to Octavian. Aristocrats watch out for each other."

James struggled to contain his surprise as he studied the three surviving members of the once illustrious Hasmonean family. The household had produced several generations of High Priests, but their glory was a thing of the past.

A famed beauty, Mariamne, at twenty-eight years of age, was sixteen years younger than Herod and the mother of four young children. Her mother, Aalexis, with her soft wrinkles and mottled complexion resembling dried rose petals, appeared harmless enough. Mariamne's grandfather, seventy-two-year-old John Hyrcanus, was a shell of a man, which was hardly a surprise.

James's stomach sickened at the gruesome recollection of the last time he had laid eyes on John Hyrcanus.

Hyrcanus had been High Priest and James new to the priesthood. Jerusalem had been rife with inner turmoil as wars were waged and the country changed hands between Rome and Persia. At the end of one such war, John Hyrcanus's nephew stole the office of High Priest from his uncle. The nation had decried the ruling that John Hyrcanus would be exiled to Persia. But the nephew proved himself worse than the wickedest of barbarians by viciously cutting off both John Hyrcanus's ears. The mutilation meant Hyrcanus could never reclaim the office of High Priest.

"If Mariamne's brother still lived, I might agree with you." Aware he was rubbing the scar on his cheek, James dropped his hand to his side.

Lightning flashed in Herod's black eyes. "The drowning was an accident."

"Of course." James scrambled to get back on safer ground. "Now about Elizabeth."

"We will get to the matter." Clearly mollified, Herod

stood and signaled for James to follow. "But first we must negotiate on a delicate subject."

James was fully prepared to cooperate if Herod asked him to act as a spy again, but hoped it would not come to that. Spying on others made him feel like a rat.

"Be prepared to be impressed."

Herod led him to a lamp-lit alcove. A white plaster model of Jerusalem took up all the space.

"Fickle Fortuna," James said, awed as a child presented with a room full of toys. "The craftsmanship is magnificent."

Herod ran his hand lovingly over a section of the city wall, the very portion constructed by his father, Antipater.

"I envision great things for Jerusalem." He stooped and hauled out a cast of a Roman-style theater from under the table, handed it to James, then dragged out the model of a hippodrome. "Where would you place them?"

James marveled at the detail. Miniature actors peopled the stage. Horse-drawn chariots raced around the oval track. "My mind is hurrying to catch up to your bold plans, but the Tyropoeon Valley would seem the natural spot for the hippodrome."

Herod grinned. "Can't you already hear the Pharisees' outrage? So we will make that our little secret for now."

"My lips are sealed." James smiled back. Keeping up with the breakneck changes of Herod's mood was exhausting.

Herod stored the small casts back under the table and moved to the far corner. Squatting to eye-level with the model, he touched the Temple roof.

"I am having a model made up of a complex two to three times larger than the present one. I welcome your suggestions."

James's palms grew sweaty. A thousand years could pass before another opportunity like this presented itself. "I could work up some drawings?"

"It goes without saying the master builder must be a Jew. One who is a priest would be even better." Herod straightened and clapped James on the back.

James froze. "This would be the *delicate* situation you mentioned?"

"You would think I asked you to start dressing like a woman." Herod laughed. "I did not say you had to embrace the conversion. Grow back your beard. Dress in priest's garments. How difficult can that be?"

Easy as slitting his own throat.

James pulled on the neck of his tunic. "I will need time to think about it."

"We both know you will agree. In the meantime, I believe I know the perfect solution for the troubling matter with Saul Boethus." Herod slung his arm around James's shoulders.

The end of the world would come before James returned to the Jewish faith. Would he be saying that if converting meant saving Elizabeth's life? If the gods were merciful, he would not ever have to learn the answer to that question.

CHAPTER 4

L ocked up alone in the stifling chamber for hours, huddled next to a sputtering lamp, Elizabeth started at the door being flung wide open.

Cold air rushed into the room as James entered, a strange look on his face. "I am sorry I was away so long."

She pushed off the wooden desk, eager to share the solution she had come up with. A plan that could solve all her problems. That was unless James carried the worst of news. She wrung her hands.

"I was able to reach a deal with King Herod."

The smell of molten metal still lingering in her nostrils, she burst into tears and her knees buckled. "Thank the Lord."

James caught her up and held her close. "You are safe. I will not allow anyone to mistreat you ever again."

"I do not know why I am crying now when it is all over." She hid her face in his tunic. "How did you win Herod to our side?"

"Perhaps we should wait until after you have rested and taken a meal to discuss the, uh...details." He stroked her back.

Something in his voice did not sit right. She broke free.

"What have you done?"

His eyes turned stormy. "You are quick to assume I am at fault."

"Tell me everything," she demanded.

A long silence passed.

"Most of the agreement should please you. King Herod *persuaded* Saul Boethus it was in his best interest to divorce you. The coward readily agreed."

She could not argue with James calling Saul a coward, nor forget the fact a cornered coward could become twice as dangerous.

"Saul would not want to risk displeasing King Herod. He was stripped of his fortune after Queen Cleopatra's death. He is eager to find a new patron."

James's face soured. "Annoyingly eager."

"You have not told me the worst yet." Unease prickled through her veins.

"I have some other good news." James's gaze slipped. "Herod has agreed to allow your brother Andrew to divorce his wife."

"I am happy for Andrew. But why would King Herod agree to the arrangement?"

James shifted guiltily but met her gaze. "Andrew insisted. In trade for agreeing to your new marriage."

Her stomach clenched. "I do not want to marry again."

"You need a husband. Someone to protect you."

She willed herself to remain calm. "I have a better answer. Help me convince Andrew to send me away to somewhere safe—and private."

"Where?" James looked briefly dumbfounded, but then shook his head. "Never mind. It does not matter because I will suggest no such thing to Andrew."

"You have not even heard my plan. I know of a small

sect of Jews in Alexandria who shelter and care for poor widows. I always admired the charity of the Agape Inn for Widows."

"You are not poor. And you are not a widow."

Frustration welled. Another unhappy marriage was too cruel a fate to consider. The divorce represented an opportunity to finally find a measure of purpose and peace.

"I would minister to the widows. Please, James, I beg you to support me in this."

"Twice I have lost you. I will not lose you again."

"Lost me? We are second cousins."

"Third cousins."

"What does this have to do with my future happiness?"

He pressed closer. "Andrew drew up a marriage contract. We are husband and wife."

The blood drained from her head. "Merciful angels, what have you done?"

"I did it for you. You need my protection."

"You are my stepson," she said, her lips numb with shock. "This is madness."

"You just need to grow accustomed to the idea."

She backed away in full panic. "King Herod and Andrew would never have suggested such a sinful arrangement. This was all your doing. Admit it."

"Yes. I love you." He trapped her against the desk. "Can you deny your feelings for me?"

"You are my stepson." Her traitorous heart warred against her sense of shame.

"In name only," he barked, his hot breath raking her face.

She was not repulsed. No, desire gnawed at her, urging her to claim his mouth and lose herself in impassioned kisses. She shoved at his chest.

"I hated this house. I hated your father. Do not push me to hate you too."

He reeled on his feet as though poleaxed. "I am not my father."

"He was cruel. This is cruel." She broke free and hurried to the door.

Ashen-faced, he followed. "I would never do anything to hurt you."

"We will be reviled wherever we go." She held up her hands, warding him off. "I will not be able to go to the Temple or anywhere in Jerusalem."

"I thought of that. I cannot shut up the gossips, but you will be welcomed at the Temple. With King Herod and High Priest Fabus and Andrew supporting your presence, the rabble will have no choice in the matter."

Another horrifying thought presented itself. "Even if you were not my stepson, you are an apostate Jew. For all I know you are worshiping pagan gods."

"Yes, I kept idols in Rome, but only for appearance's sake. Jewish or pagan, I consider religion utter nonsense."

"I refuse to acknowledge the marriage." She crossed her arms and lifted her chin.

"King Herod will be holding a banquet a week from now in honor of our union. You will be there."

"You would do this against my will?" Tears stung her eyes.

His mouth twisted. He ripped open the door and banged it closed behind him, leaving a deafening silence.

Elizabeth slumped onto the floor and pressed her forehead to her drawn-up knees. Did James have no compassion? Herod had killed her father. And now he expected her to smile while Herod blessed this sinful marriage.

◆ ◆ ◆

A short while later she jumped at the soft knock on the reception chamber door. She scrambled to her feet. Her heart pounded harder. She scrubbed her hot eyes. Tears were a luxury she could not afford. The accusation of adultery and the marriage to James spelled her ruin.

Angels in heaven, she needed to think this through.

She must find a way to escape. Escape James. Escape Jerusalem. Escape more heartache and shame.

She backed away as the door creaked open. She would demand James take her to Andrew's home—the very same house where her parents had raised her and her three brothers.

Would she be welcomed?

Andrew had never treated her with kindness. Zealous in guarding his ritual purity, he had resented her presence. She was no longer *zavah*, but it would not make a difference. Andrew had proved that earlier today, by failing to intercede on her behalf at her trial, and by his eagerness to see her executed.

Andrew was not the answer.

She could write to Gabriel. It would be unfair to burden him with her troubles. He was already caring for their sick mother and had his own family to see after.

Another knock on the door, louder this time.

She pulled the door open. "James, I insist you send me to the Agape Inn for Wido—"

A rheumy-eyed serving man limped into the room blinking in confusion. "Master James asked me to help you settle into the bedchamber."

She crossed her arms. James could not possibly believe she would go willingly to the marriage bed. Or that he would send a slave to do his dirty work. And an elderly one at that. A kind master would have freed the man long ago. This further example of James's selfishness galled. "May I ask your name?"

"I am called Saad." The slave smiled beatifically. "Do you prefer to be called Mistress Elizabeth?"

She did not plan on being in this wretched place long enough to be on friendly terms with the household. "Where is James? I would like to speak to him."

"Master James went to the upper market to purchase new tunics and nice smelling soap for you. He said something about procuring special herbs."

Saad shuffled to the door, clearly expecting her to follow.

Trailing the slave, she slowed. James was making sure she would have her cure. It irritated her that he could be thoughtful and thoughtless at the same time.

They emerged from the narrow hall into the drafty entryway. The gray walls and floor could not have been more cheerless. The musty air was not quite as thick here.

Grim memories arose of Simeon Onias's shrill, hateful voice echoing through the house.

She rubbed her chilled arms. "Has the house been empty these last eight years?"

Saad paused at the bottom of the steep stairway and exhaled wearily.

"Master James mentioned selling the place a few times. But nothing ever came of it. You will be happy to hear, the bedchambers have been scrubbed cleaned and aired out."

The thought of being prisoned in Simeon's home repulsed and sickened.

She turned on her heel and fought to open the main door to the house.

"Where are you going?" Saad called, aghast.

She did not know. She did not care. But she could not stay. Not here.

She fled outside and crashed into James.

He caught her up in his arms, saving her from falling. Concern and surprise written on his face, he examined her for bodily harm. "Libi, what is wrong?"

"Wrong? Everything is wrong." She struggled against his strong hold. "You should not be calling me Libi. We should not be married. This house is the last place I want to live."

A one-armed slave boy carrying James's purchases waddled sideways into the house. Next door, the elderly priest Jachim watched them from his front steps in the company of his grandsons.

James released her but kept a firm grip on her wrist. He offered her an earnest look. "I hate this house more than you. I plan to knock down every last stone and replace it with the loveliest home wealth can buy. In the meantime, I'd just as soon finish this conversation inside, out of sight of our neighbors."

She released a shaky breath. The chance to escape had passed.

"Fine, you win. For now."

He led her inside, "Go," he commanded, sending the slaves hastening out of sight.

His frustration with her filled the gloomy entryway. "Just where did you think you were going?"

She fisted her hands, but acknowledged his point had merit.

"I suppose I would have found someone to take me or

gone to Gabriel's farm in Galilee. My brother would never turn me away. If Leonidas had a regular home, he would welcome me as well."

"Your brothers are good and honorable, but did you stop to imagine the grief they would suffer if you failed to escape and were instead caught and stoned to death by an angry mob. Worse, you could have fallen into the hands of the Roman garrison."

A worried look creased his forehead. "Libi, you have to promise me you will not put a foot outside unless I am with you."

"I will not act rashly again." Her stomach revolted, and her knees weakened as she realized the risk of being ravaged by Roman soldiers.

James offered his arm for support.

She straightened and lifted her chin. Her agreement was sensible, but she would not have him misconstrue it for a surrender.

"I will remain because I must. But the marriage is one in name only, until other arrangements can be made."

He shot her a formidable glare. "Or until you grow used to the idea."

"I will not *grow* used to the idea."

"And if I insist you share my bed?"

"You would not take me against my will."

He smoothed his tunic. "I plan to bend your will to mine."

"You are as bad as your father. Forever scheming and plotting."

He reared back as though struck. "I am nothing like my father."

"Act differently if you do not care for the comparison."

She got no joy from hurting him. Why did he have to

push her until she lashed out? She would not be surprised if he refused her the last favor she had to ask.

"I desire to be reunited with my dearest friend Apollo."

"Apollo?" A jealous glint flashed in James's black eyes.

"My cat."

"A cat?"

Under other circumstances his baffled expression would be highly entertaining. "I would be grateful if someone could be sent to collect Apollo from Saul and Phaedra."

CHAPTER 5

Not fit for company after Libi's charge he was acting like his father, James put off the task of claiming the cat for several hours.

The one-armed slave boy Marcus fidgeted as they waited in the reception chamber of Saul Boethus's rented home.

"Jerusalem does not amount to a pimple on Rome's backside," Marcus remarked, in his ongoing campaign to disparage James's decision to desert Rome for Jerusalem.

"I cannot argue with your astute observation, but your constant chattering to return to Rome is not easing my headache. Perhaps it would have been kinder to find you a new master."

The ten-year-old shook his head with vigor. "No. I am very happy with you. I am sure I will learn to love everything about Jerusalem."

"No one is asking you to love it," James assured the boy. He would grant Marcus his freedom when he was old enough to fend for himself. "But if you do not stop talking I might have to command you to pick lint from my tunics or some other drab chore."

Eyes bright with a smile, Marcus sealed his lips. Then

like most boys his age, his attention moved on. He was rocking on his heels and humming, as he studied the peeling red and gold cornice trimming the ceiling.

James pinched the bridge of his nose. Patience. He needed more patience.

Here, at least, was proof he was not his father. Simeon Onias excelled at making slaves quake. The hateful man had called James weak and softhearted, or worse, because he allowed his slaves to maintain a measure of dignity.

Fickle Fortuna, see what your accusation has done to me, Libi? A face-to-face meeting with Saul Boethus was not the place for second-guessing himself.

"*Shalom*, James Onias," Saul said with annoying calm, strolling through an arched entryway, accompanied by a slave carrying a large black and white cat. Two more slaves carried an opulent travel chest, presumably stuffed with Elizabeth's belongings.

Taking the man's use of the Hebrew greeting as a good sign, James nonetheless balled his hands. "Suddenly embracing your Jewishness is convenient. If I replied with my own Jewish blessing, that would make us the two biggest hypocrites in Jerusalem."

Saul's orange-tinted lips pursed briefly before curling with a smile. "You have your strategy for winning King Herod's favor, and I have mine."

That Elizabeth had been married to this womanish man sickened James.

"Allow me to give you some advice. You will need to give up painting your face to have any hope of being accepted in Jerusalem."

Saul dabbed a purple square of cloth to his nose. "And you should bathe more frequently. Going around smelling worse than a salt mine slave will not win you friends."

James sniffed an armpit. "My stonecutter friends would not agree with your assessment."

Saul was not amused. "Please be so kind as to tell Elizabeth I do not hold a grudge. Aside from this one incident, she was an exemplary wife."

"How charitable of you," James growled, still quaking in his sandals at Elizabeth's close brush with death, and a brutal death at that. "Why the change of heart?"

"My sister and I agree that Jonah was wholly at fault. He was my brother-in-law for less than six months. We were unaware of his unstable character, which grew steadily worse with the move to Jerusalem. Something must have made him snap. Assure Elizabeth that Phaedra and I will proclaim her innocence before all."

Something about the confession did not sit right with James, but he could not put his finger on the problem. "What are you hoping to gain?"

Saul smiled from behind the perfumed cloth and waved for his slave to hand over the cat.

"I will join you in offering some friendly advice. Take Elizabeth and start over somewhere else."

"That will not happen." Especially since viewing the model of Jerusalem and learning of King Herod's grand plans for the city. Not taking his eyes off Saul, James reached for the black and white cat.

A twinkling glint shone in Saul's black-lined eyes. "I am surprised King Herod has not heard of the unfortunate *accident* at your last work site."

The cat hissed and struggled to escape. James hugged the animal. Dagger-like claws dug in his chest. "Hell and damnation, Marcus, take this infernal beast before I do something I regret."

James winced as the claws were sucked from his chest.

"Apollo," Marcus cooed. "You will find Master James agreeable once you get to know him."

The cat curled into the crook of the boy's lone arm.

A stone worker's assistant, Marcus had lost his arm the day a two-story wall collapsed. But the tragedy was no accident—a competitor of James's had paid the newly hired foreman to use inferior mortar. The boy continued to show remarkable courage and determination in the months since the accident.

With such an example before him, James could hardly feel bitter over the rival master builder succeeding in his goal to inflict harm on James's reputation. With no new projects or contracts in sight, James had had no choice but to abandon Rome and accept King Herod's invitation.

The cat's contented purr filled the silence. An icy ball formed in James's stomach. Libi's cat would have a new owner if James had not been here to halt her execution.

He narrowed his eyes. "I would be surprised if King Herod did not know about the accident. He has a network of spies from here to Rome. Which means he knows everything there is to know about you."

Saul's smile did not falter. "I have nothing to hide."

One thing was certain—James was well on his way to hating Saul Boethus as much as when they were boys.

CHAPTER 6

Vials filled with ointments, healing herbs, and liquid cures clinked and rattled in the reed basket Avda Hama's sixteen-year-old son Ori carried. Avda's steps slowed as he entered the women's private reception chamber.

The newly renovated winter palace in Jericho was many times larger than the Hasmonean palace in Jerusalem. Frescoes of the quality found in Rome or Egypt adorned every wall. The white and gold mosaic tiled floors dazzled. The Roman-inspired palace-fortress was not like any other in Israel, which was fitting as Herod of Idumea was not like any ruler who had come before.

However, fear and uncertainty gripped the winter palace as King Herod awaited the summons that would take him to Rhodes to face the judgment of the current Roman ruler, Octavian. Edgy from the wait, Herod had made a snap decision to relocate to Jericho, but the upheaval left the entire household feeling frayed and jumpy.

"Her Grandness is rubbing her forehead," Ori whispered as they neared the formal arrangement of gilded couches where Herod's mother Cypros and various nieces, cousins, and daughters of dignitaries sat.

Queen Mariamne and her mother and their contingent of female relatives and acquaintances occupied the other half of the room. Children babbled and played at the women's feet.

Cypros's headaches always gave Avda one. "Her Grandness wanted to meet her son in private, but the king insisted the women gather to bid farewell to him and the hunting party."

"Do you wish you were going on the hunting trip with Herod?" Ori asked.

His oldest son had recently shed his baby face, and his voice was deepening. Hama wished his first wife had lived to see her son begin his training as a physician. Mary always said Ori took after him. It was difficult to believe his sweet lively Mary had been dead for fourteen years.

"Would you like to learn to hunt?" Hama replied, steeling himself to wade in among the gathered women. Herod's hunting trips held no appeal to him. But it might be safer than entering this den of lionesses.

Ori shook his head and poked at the bottles filling the medicine basket. "Will you use your new pain cure?"

Avda squeezed his son's slender shoulder. "I will tell you the same my father said to me and his father said to him the day I took up the practice of medicine...kindness and patience work as many wonders as salves and potions."

Ori stared back, his large brown eyes too serious. "I would rather be a teacher."

Avda blinked. "A teacher?"

"Of the Law," the boy clarified. "Benjamin likes to watch you crush and mix the medicines. You could tutor him to be a physician and I could study to be a teacher."

Much as Avda loved Benjamin, he doubted the rambunctious fourteen-year-old had the patience for the long years of study and discipline required of physicians.

"I remember being nervous and unsure the first time I acted as assistant to my father," Avda said, guiding Ori to her Grandness.

Descended from Nabatean royalty, Cypros ceased massaging her forehead. Her once perfect olive skin had faded to a dull mustard yellow. "Physician Hama, where have you been? I called for you over an hour ago."

Long accustomed to Cypros's imperious manner, Avda lifted a green bottle from the basket Ori clutched to his chest. He winked at Ori, hoping to ease his son's skittishness. "My son and I had our heads together making a new cure."

Cypros almost managed a smile. "My dear husband always said you were the finest physician this side of the Great Sea."

The *new cure* was a thyme mixture touted as remedy for those suffering from gloomy moods. Avda did not know if the herbal remedy would alleviate Cypros's sufferings, but it would not cause her any harm either. He handed the potion to the slave girl hovering behind the woman's shoulder. "Mix two drops into her Grandness's wine each morning and evening."

Cypros snapped her fingers. "Show Physician Hama the picture the messenger delivered yesterday."

The slave girl scurried to obey.

Queen Mariamne glanced up from her needlework and wrinkled her elegant nose at her mother-in-law. "Physician Hama can do better than the daughter of an Idumean goat herder."

Cypros glared back indignantly. "The king's cousin would make a perfectly acceptable wife for a physician.

Rafa is a lovely girl."

Avda's chest tightened. The loss of two wives before his thirty-ninth birthday had given Avda enough grief to last a lifetime.

Ori hugged the bottle-filled basket and moved closer to Avda. Chaya's sudden death just one year ago had been difficult for him and his sons.

A charcoal drawing of a sweet-faced girl close to the same age as Ori was offered for inspection. Avda waved away the small square of parchment.

Deliberately misunderstanding, he said, "I'm sure Rafa is a wonderful girl, but Ori will not take a wife until he finishes his studies."

"Rafa will join my court." Cypros straightened on her thin-cushioned couch. "Take six more months to calm your feelings, then you must marry. Married physicians make better healers than unmarried men."

Queen Mariamne offered Avda a sympathetic frown. "And everyone knows what soothing wives the women from my dear husband's family make."

"I come from the royal family of Nabatea," Cypros replied. "My blood is every bit as good as yours."

Avda clapped his hands, claiming the women's attention. King Herod was under enough strain without having to walk into the latest contentious argument between his wife and mother. They stared at him expectantly. For the most part he liked Cypros and Queen Mariamne and tried to avoid being dragged into their differences.

Ignorant of the tension, the children continued with their cheerful play.

Ori nudged his elbow, then tapped the stopper on the small vial of poppy extract.

Avda grinned at the private jest. After particularly turbulent days, Avda would drop into his seat inside his comfortable set of rooms and claim that giving everyone a dose of poppy extract was the only way he would ever know a moment's rest from the tumult constantly swirling inside Herod's household.

But he had known what he was getting into when he accepted the position of royal physician. It was the least he could do to repay King Herod for sheltering and protecting him, Ori and Benjamin when Jerusalem was conquered by Parthia. Many of Herod's supporters died during those dark days.

Praise the Lord his children were strong and healthy. Everything else was a mere aggravation. He returned his attention to Cypros and Queen Mariamne. "I recommend taking in some fresh air among the gardens and pools later this morning. You will feel remarkably re—"

"Of course I would find good Physician Hama pushing his favorite cure of exercise and fresh air," a familiar flirtatious voice said, followed by a tinkling laugh Avda would recognize anywhere.

He turned and found the vivacious Kitra waving a greeting. One of the many nieces Cypros had taken in over the years, Kitra was by far the most untamed and beautiful.

Awash in flaming sunlight, Kitra held tight to the hand of her four-year-old daughter, who shared the same almond eyes and glossy black hair as her mother.

Avda cleared his throat. "Welcome to the palace. I had not heard you would be visiting your aunt."

The polished double doors behind Kitra snapped closed. "The trip was a hurried affair." Her smile had a fragile quality that awakened his protective instincts.

He moved toward her. "Are you feeling poorly?"

"I am a bit tired from the journey," Kitra hastened to say, clearly not wanting him to make a fuss.

Avda halted. Unease prickled like diamond dust over his skin. "When you are recovered you will have to introduce me to your beautiful little girl."

Many years had passed since Avda had last seen Kitra, when she'd been a mere girl of seventeen. Her showy looks had given way to the exotic beauty for which the women in her family were famed. She had been married for a brief time to James Onias. Avda never learned why the marriage failed, but Kitra remarried shortly thereafter to a prince from Nabatea. The prince would be the young girl's father.

"My granddaughter's name is Jazmine," Cypros said, her voice full of irritation at being left out of the conversation.

Her Grandness would be doubly unhappy if she knew Avda had forgotten she, or anyone else, was in the room. He raked his fingers through his hair. "Jazmine and Kitra look as though they are in need of food and sleep."

"My father sent us away," the child announced in a singsong voice, staring up at the rosette-adorned ceiling.

Scarlet bloomed on Kitra's cheeks. "Hush, darling."

Jazmine broke free from her mother and skipped around the base of a pink sandstone column. "Father dis...in...hated me."

"Disowned you," Kitra corrected gently, then pulled a small doll from a woven, coral-colored sack, and led her daughter back to the center of the chamber.

Pity for Kitra's plight tightened Avda's chest. What a terrible blow this must be to her. She had been raised to use her beauty and womanly wiles to twist men's hearts in the direction she chose.

Cypros clucked her tongue. "Your father is most unhappy."

Queen Mariamne stared with open fascination.

Red lips trembling, Kitra lifted her chin. "I was told my father would be arriving shortly from Idumea."

"I fear your fate will be the same as my dear sister," Cypros said. "Exile to the Salt Sea has been extremely difficult on your mother."

Kitra swallowed. "I will speak to my brother. Father always heeds Taj."

Avda admired Kitra's bravery, but feared she was close to collapse. He moved to her side and cupped her elbow. She was much too thin but did not smell of sickness. Of course, it was difficult to judge accurately over the alluring perfume she favored.

"You should rest," he said in her ear.

She leaned more heavily on his arm. "I think it will be a long time before I know a restful moment."

He could not solve her problems, but Kitra would not sicken for lack of sleep and food. Not if he had anything to say about it.

"Have Kitra and Jazmine's belongings sent to the white room," Avda instructed Cypros. The plainest chamber in the palace, the white room was set aside for patients under his care.

Cypros's brow wrinkled. "Kitra has not fully explained herself."

"Stay and have your noon meal with us," Queen Mariamne said, her interest in Kitra a little too keen.

King Herod was an acclaimed soldier, and the women of his household were no less warriors. The difference was that the women fought their battles in the grand halls of the palace. Avda would ensure Kitra had a respite from prying eyes and uncomfortable questions, giving her a chance to recover her strength before taking on Cypros and Queen Mariamne again.

"Explanations will have to wait," Avda said respectfully but firmly, leading Kitra and Jazmine away.

Ori followed, his basket of bottles rattling over the hum of dismay swirling through the women's entourage.

Kitra gazed at him, a vulnerable look in her eyes. "You have always been unfailingly kind."

Most people considered Kitra silly and vain, but the cloth sack draped over her shoulder and modest dress were a far cry from her usual flashy beads and provocative clothes. Her tenderness with Jazmine was touching and indicated she might no longer be so selfish and self-centered.

"Assisting others is bred into my blood," he said.

What he could not explain was why Kitra had always held a fond spot in his heart and why he did not want her to guess at his feelings.

CHAPTER 7

An hour after arriving at King Herod's winter palace, Kitra paced the milk-white chamber Physician Hama had graciously provided. Pausing beside one of the narrow beds, she tucked the soft blanket around Jazmine. Lips a perfect rosebud and black fly-away hair fanning the snowy white pillow, Jazmine slumbered peacefully, unaware of their perilous situation.

Crumbs covered the bedside table—the remnants of their noon meal. Her little girl would never want for food or shelter, thanks to her family's fabulous wealth. But if Kitra did not act quickly, she and Jazmine might be shunted off to a dreary, prison-like existence. It would be the same fate suffered by her mother, who had been her father's chief wife, but was presently languishing in a desert fortress overlooking the Salt Sea. A fate Kitra had sworn would never be hers.

Her failure to please her prince-husband was a spectacular disaster. A prince. She had been married to a prince. Prince Obodas's divorce and repudiation of Jazmine brought shame on her, shame on her father's name, and shame on the family name.

Kitra wanted to claw out the eyes of the person who had turned her husband against her and Jazmine. Prince Obodas had been putty in her hands until someone had poisoned his mind.

Jazmine stirred.

"Mama will fight to her last breath to win back favor with Grandfather." Kitra brushed a soft kiss across her cheek.

"Motherhood agrees with you," a gentle voice said.

"Physician Hama." Kitra stood. Feeling more like herself for having traded her rumpled travel garment for her favorite sheer sleeping gown, she tucked a frizzy strand of hair behind her ear, ran her hands over her hips, and giggled. "Shame on you for sneaking up on me."

Physician Hama set aside his basket of medicines, grabbed a blanket from the second bed, and wrapped it around her shoulders. Though past his fortieth birthday, Avda Hama still retained a well-built, powerful body. Kind brown eyes softened a square-jawed face. "You do not have to act flirtatious for my benefit."

The reprimand stung. "If I was trying to seduce you, I promise you would not be in any doubt of it."

"I did not intend to insult you." He patted her arm. "I know you fawn and preen over men because you think that is what they—"

The judgment of others usually did not matter to her. "Fawn? Preen?" She batted his hand away.

He arched a brow.

"Fuddled men are easier to deal with."

He smiled, clearly amused. "Most people underestimate you."

Exile awaited her if she failed to win over her father, brother, Herod, or some other man of importance to her cause.

"I dearly hope so."

"Can I help?" Sympathy shone in Physician Hama's eyes.

Though she needed a friend in the palace, Kitra liked and respected Physician Hama too much to do wrong by him. He had a good heart, but he might not be so generous if he knew the secret involving her brother Taj and Physician Hama's second wife.

She wrapped the blanket tighter around her body and noticed the lines of grief marring his face. "You have had your own troubles to contend with."

"Chaya was shy and quiet, but I think you would have liked her."

His obvious love for his wife was admirable and hardened her resolve to resist the offer of help.

"You are not sleeping well," she scolded. "You need to stop worrying over others and start caring for yourself. Mix a sleeping potion at bedtime. You are a physician, after all. Now go find someone else to fuss over."

He could not have looked more startled. He pointed to his basket of cures. "Can I fix—"

"Go away," she said, waving her hands in a shooing motion, wishing she was wearing her bangles. She delighted in the jangling noise they made, even as they lulled others into dismissing her as silly and harmless.

"Jazmine does not know how blessed she is to have you as her mother."

Tears sprang to Kitra's eyes. Men had always showered her in flattery, but none of those compliments had ever touched her heart. "Stop talking nonsense. I—"

A knock sounded at the door and a red-headed servant entered. "Faakhir Aretas would like an audience with his daughter."

Kitra's heart sped and her stomach knotted. She glanced at the travel chest holding her gowns and jewels.

"Tell my father to expect me shortly."

"I can speak to your father," Hama said, touching the blanket draping her shoulders. "Tell him you are unwell. Take more time to recover from your flight from Nabatea to Jericho."

More tired than she cared to admit, she slipped out of the blanket, walked with swaying hips to the filigree-decorated chest, then cast a sultry look back over her shoulder. "Leave, unless you would like to watch me dress."

Physician Hama's cheeks flamed. "I wish you success."

"You are a sweet man." Taking it as a good sign she had managed to fluster the stoic physician, she winked.

Mumbling under his breath, he grabbed up his basket of cures and departed posthaste. As the clinking of the medicine bottles faded to silence, Kitra took a deep breath in preparation for putting on the best performance of her life.

CHAPTER 8

Heart jangling louder than her bracelets, Kitra glided into her father's private quarters, the most lavish suite the winter palace had to offer. Her father's current chief wife, Haabeel, and her three equally beautiful daughters smiled maliciously from plush reclining couches. Of marriageable age, her half-sisters were bedecked in clingy jewel-colored gowns that glittered in the sunlight pouring through the tall arched windows.

Father and six of his sons stood around an immense platform bed. Plump red pillows had been tossed aside, and an array of bows, arrows, knives, and spears were strewn over the red and gold striped cover.

"Kitra, what took you so long?" Haabeel accused. "The men are eager to join King Herod's hunting expedition."

Her half-brothers frowned in Kitra's direction, then returned to admiring the arsenal of weapons.

Deep in discussion with his oldest son, Taj, Father did not acknowledge her.

Taj eyed her with amusement. Gorgeously handsome, Taj had inherited their mother's elegant straight nose. Kitra shared a special bond with Taj that she did not enjoy with her twenty-three half siblings conceived by Father's four other wives.

At the moment she wanted to strangle Taj over his delight in watching her squirm. "You wanted to see me, Father." She hated the insecure tone in her voice.

Father did not hear her, or worse, ignored her. "Which dagger do you favor for skinning deer?" Father asked Taj.

Taj winked at her, then picked out a short-handled dagger for Father's inspection.

Father stroked the glistening blade.

Not about to be ignored in favor of shiny toys, Kitra moistened her painted lips and sauntered across the room. "Father, you have grown more handsome and distinguished."

Tall, refined, and graying at the temples, her father smiled warmly and tossed the dagger onto the bed. "Kitra, my beautiful dove. Is Physician Hama taking good care of you?"

Captured in her father's bear-like embrace, she was comforted by the familiar fragrance of rich, dark spices. "We were provided with enough food to feed an army."

He kissed her forehead. "Where is Jazmine? I hoped to see my granddaughter before departing for the hunt."

Relief washed through Kitra. "She is asleep. But I could —"

"No, no," he said with a laugh. "If I have learned one thing over the years, it is never to wake a sleeping child." He set her at arm's length, and his smile faded. "Explain what happened, my dove."

"Did Prince Obodas grow tired of you?" Haabeel interjected, voice rich with satisfaction.

Kitra's confidence shattered like a vase pushed from a shelf, and she was transformed into the little girl who could not get enough time and attention from her larger-than-life father.

She clasped his strong hands. "Come for a walk in the gardens. We can talk there."

"You are fortunate Prince Obodas did not have you beheaded." Father extracted his hands, and Haabeel smiled her satisfaction.

"Prince Obodas turned on me without warning. If you speak to him, he might—"

"I expected better from you, Daughter."

Kitra dug her fingernails into her palms. "Several of the prince's brothers were always making eyes at me. I am sure I—"

"You are finished in Nabatea," Father said, his voice brisk and business-like. "I am going to send you to your mother until I decide what to do about you."

Panic arose, and she was tempted to fall prostrate at his feet and grovel and beg for mercy, but she inhaled a steadying breath.

Taj moved to her side and put a supportive arm around her waist. "Allow Kitra to stay here with Aunt Cypros and she will catch you a son-in-law greater than Prince Obodas. She will win the affections of King Herod."

Stunned silence greeted the breathtaking proposal, then gave way to a buzz of speculation among her half brothers and sisters.

Father folded his arms and tapped his lip. "Herod and Kitra...now that has possibilities."

Seduce Herod? "Kitra's stomach pitched. She was not opposed to making men salivate with lust, but she had never stolen another woman's husband.

"Queen Mariamne already hates our family."

Haabeel hopped from her couch like a bird chased

from its nest. "Kitra is an old used sandal. Herod will not look twice at her. Not when he could have a beautiful young virgin. My Darah will seduce Herod."

Kitra, at twenty-three, was considered past her prime. Indignant, she flapped her hand and took comfort in the tinkling of her bracelets.

"Why send a child to do a woman's task?"

Taj skimmed his hand along her curves. "Many men prefer an experienced partner."

Kitra slapped his hand. "I will not be Herod's plaything. I will be his wife."

"You believe you can win Herod over?" Father said, giving Kitra the sharp attention usually reserved for his sons.

She would not admit that she was a bit frightened of Herod. A formidable soldier and statesman, with a reputation for ruthlessness, Herod had taken many lovers and would not hesitate to execute a man or woman he believed betrayed him or tricked him. Seduction would require a subtle touch.

Taj pressed his mouth to her ear. "Mother and Jazmine are depending on you."

What her brother hoped to gain from Kitra risking all was a mystery, but he was correct. This was her opportunity to redeem her mother from exile and to save herself and Jazmine from a similar fate. She would take her chances with Herod rather than risk oblivion.

Throat dry as the Nabatean desert, she flashed a brilliant smile. "You will have Herod for a son-in-law before the winter is out."

Father smiled approvingly.

All would be lost if Kitra failed to capture Herod's interest.

But she could not and would not fail.

CHAPTER 9

Gathered with the king's household among the luxury and comfort of the sparkling new pool complex, Avda reclined on his couch, enjoying the sight of his sons splashing in the cool clear water.

The sound of a girlish giggle claimed his attention.

He glanced at the far end of the pool where red-lipped Kitra sat with her tunic hiked, exposing shapely lily-white legs, as she kicked water at the young men ogling her generous curves.

Tempted to demand she exchange her sheer, clingy gown for a thick robe, Avda scrubbed his face. "She wants you to stare," he scolded himself. Every time he caught sight of her since her arrival at the palace one week ago, he found himself mesmerized anew.

Jazmine skipped to her mother's side. Kitra hugged the girl, then removed Jazmine's sandals and coaxed her to kick her feet in the water.

Avda admired the time and attention Kitra poured on Jazmine, but winced at her teaching her daughter to copy her flirtatious ways. He was not the only one unhappy. Queen Mariamne glared from the palm-shaded alcove where she lounged with her mother, children, and extended Hasmonean family.

Kitra was breaking several unspoken rules. First, she'd invaded the queen's territory. The design of the pool complex, featuring twin pools and private sitting areas separated by gardens, served as a natural barrier between King Herod's Idumean family and Queen Mariamne's Hasmonean family.

The difference between the feuding factions could not have been more distinct. Mingled laughter and boisterous shouts came from the pool presided over by her Grandness Cypros as both young men and women frolicked in the water.

The Hasmoneans were more subdued with only the men enjoying the waters. That was until Kitra arrived in all her siren glory to mesmerize Mariamne's nephews— her second offense. The sporting between the men and women would fuel the chatter circulating Jerusalem of the lurid goings-on at the new pools and Roman bath. *Nude bathing, drunken revelry, wild orgies,* the gossips were whispering.

True, most Jerusalemites would consider men lounging and swimming in the pools in only their loincloths in full view of the women scandalous. But the winter palace was far from a house of ill-repute. Nudity was confined to the indoor bath, and as far as Avda knew, men and women did not bathe together. Wine and food did flow generously, but decorum reigned in the banquet halls and palace grounds. Herod was not the barbarian or the filthy heathen of his enemies' imaginings.

Of course, the king did not help his cause by building palaces mimicking the comforts and lifestyle of Rome. Avda wished he would do more to win favor with the people, instead of insisting they learn to accept and embrace foreign ways. But concern for the delicate religious feelings of his countrymen was not Herod's strength.

Recently arrived from Nabatea, Kitra would not fully understand the rat's nest of tension she had stumbled into.

"Come swim," Benjamin called.

Making plans to have a heart-to-heart talk with Kitra, Avda nodded at his son and gripped the wax tablet he used to jot down descriptions of diseases and preparations for cures. "Let me finish my notes first."

Benjamin made a face but went back to wrestling with his older brother and young Antipater.

Avda tapped the stylus against the wood frame of the tablet and smiled watching his sons roughhousing in the pool with Herod's oldest son.

Ori and Antipater were nearly the same age. Antipater, with his dark skin and large white teeth, was the image of his father, and was as aggressive and bullheaded as Herod had been that age. Antipater was already putting on muscle, outweighing tall and slender Ori by a hefty amount.

Ori's quickness helped him to hold his own against Antipater. Benjamin was doing his best to keep up with the older boys, repeatedly refusing to abandon the water fight when asked if he was ready to surrender.

It was high time Antipater joined his father. The boy and his mother had been living in seclusion in one of Herod's desert fortresses with no one to champion their cause.

Avda glanced again at vivacious, provocative Kitra. She was in the fight of her life against men who held all the power. Women had few weapons to call upon. Was it fair to blame her for using her allure to her advantage?

Herod emerged from the nearby gardens. Changing the air of anyplace he entered, he moved with the slow grace of a lion surveying his pride.

He stopped beside Avda. Tanned and refreshed after the week-long hunting trip, he grinned down at the boys. "Reminds me of when we were their age, and you were always trying to keep up with me and my brothers."

Ori, Benjamin, and Antipater shouted greetings, then returned to their fun.

Avda fished his sandals from beneath the reclining couch, slipped his feet into them, and stood. Five years younger than Herod, the two had practically been raised as brothers. But Herod becoming king had changed everything.

"The gardens and pools are magnificent."

Herod brushed fingers through his woolly hair, erasing the crease where his crown rested, and gazed at the stately columns, Roman-style bathhouse, and sunken gardens.

"Not a bad bit of work for a grizzled soldier and former governor of Galilee."

Although proud and impressed with how far Herod had advanced the fortunes of the family in a span of fifteen years, Avda still found it difficult to believe this warrior had managed to become king.

"Your father and Phasael and Joseph would rejoice to see what you have done."

The pain and devastation wrought by the murder of his father and brothers lingered in Herod's black eyes. "They should be here."

The words brought the faces of Mary and Chaya to Avda's mind. If he had been a better physician, they might still be alive. He suspected Herod partly blamed himself for the death of his father and brothers.

Avda nodded at their sons. "All we can do now is make sure they have a secure future."

"Actually, that is why I sought you out. I need your help with a small matter."

"Can it wait a short while?" Avda glanced at his sons.

Herod laughed. "Let me guess. You promised the boys you would swim with them."

"You will be king until we are both old men. They will not be boys for much longer."

The gleam in Herod's eyes dimmed. "You realize my enemies are working tirelessly to take my head and my crown?" Not waiting for a response, he exhaled heavily. "Meet me in my antechamber when you are through." Then he strode away.

"Are you coming?" Benjamin asked, his voice hopeful.

Avda shook away the weight of the ever-present palace troubles, removed his sandals, and dipped a toe in the pool. Cool, clear water provided by a mountain-fed aqueduct lapped against blue-green tiles. "Suppose you and I take on Ori and Antipater in a water-fight-to-end-all-water-fights rematch."

Benjamin hopped in place and clapped. "We will win this time. I know we will."

Ori and Antipater thrashed through the water, fighting their way to the younger boy.

"No you won't," Ori called.

Antipater pounded the water with his fists. "We will crush you."

Avda loosened the belt of his striped linen robe, checked his loincloth to make sure it was secure, and shrugged the robe from his shoulders. His eyes went to Kitra, who was still sitting at the edge of the pool with

Jazmine splashing and playing nearby. Even as he wondered what had promoted the impulse, he found Kitra watching him, eyes sparkling with appreciation.

She hugged her lovely legs to her chest, rested her chin on her knees, and continued to study him.

Heat flared, awakening desires he thought dead and buried with Chaya. *Infernal flames.* Why Kitra? Of all the woman in Israel, why her? She wasn't anything like Mary or Chaya. Then again, that might be reason enough.

Avda plunged into the cool waters. The boys whooped and hollered at the wall of water he sent crashing over them. But he could not enjoy the play.

Ashamed and angry with himself and Kitra, he would put a stop to her dangerous flirtations. And do it sooner rather than later.

CHAPTER 10

Moments after leaving Jazmine with a cousin and exiting the oasis of the pools, Kitra caught up to Herod and his guardsmen in the long colonnade leading to his private chambers.

"Your Highness," she called, her heart pounding so loud she feared he would hear the echo dancing off the polished white columns. The distaste for seducing another woman's husband arose again. But she had promised Father she would win Herod's favor.

Dark eyes flashed with danger and power. He regarded her for a long moment, then sent his men ahead.

"Kitra, what may I do for you, my fair cousin?"

Run, run far, far away, her mind screamed.

Though their mothers were sisters, Herod was many years her senior. She could be facing a worse fate. Among the royal and high priestly families uncles regularly married young nieces as a mean of securing family wealth. Herod's sister Salome had been married to an uncle. Kitra shuddered at the thought of being the wife to one of her old, fat uncles.

"My wish is to please you." She smiled invitingly.

Broad shouldered and muscled, Herod wasn't unattractive. He arched a thick brow. "How dangerous do you like your games?"

"Very dangerous," she said, using a breathy voice.

His glittering black gaze moved lower. The cold draft racing down the hall molded her gauzy gold gown to her curves. He drew closer and traced a calloused finger down her bodice. "Prove it."

Her courage wavered for an instant. But it was either seduce Herod or be exiled to the Salt Sea. She directed his hand to her bottom, rose on her toes, and bit his lip.

He growled like a feral cat and kissed her, forcing his tongue into her mouth.

He tasted of onion and liver and aggression. She groaned as if pleasured, but feared her cousin would not be generous or kind in bed.

Laughing, Herod ended the kiss and released her. "My physician does not look happy with us."

She twisted around.

Like an angry god carved from marble, Physician Hama filled the hall entrance.

Her face heated. "Are you following me?"

"Do not shift the blame to me." He stormed to them.

She pointed in the direction of the pools. "Go back to your own affairs."

Herod clapped Physician Hama on the back. "Do not allow a friendly kiss between cousins to upset you."

Physician Hama crossed his arms tightly over his chest. "I know what I saw."

"Leave off scolding poor Kitra and come to my antechamber." Chuckling, Herod strolled away.

"I will be with you shortly," Physician Hama said through clenched teeth.

He fixed his molten gaze on Kitra. "What game are you

playing this time?"

The conquest of Herod would require all her *talents*. Physician Hama's disappointment and judgment was a burden and a distraction she did not need.

"You worry more than ten grandmothers."

"Someone has to. Does your father think so little of you to whore you to Herod?"

She slapped his face.

He grasped her wrist. "There has to be another way." A red welt blazed his cheek.

"I am doing what I must to survive and to secure Jazmine's future. Why do you care?"

His brown eyes resembled the turbulent muddy waters of the Jordan River. "You are a strong woman. You have more to offer a man than your body."

Was she strong? What would become of her once her skin wrinkled and her curves sagged? Who would love her then?

Exposed and lonely and vulnerable, she lifted her chin. "Is that a kind way of saying I am growing to be an old crone?"

His laughter rumbled like water tumbling over stones, making him look ten years younger. "You have nothing to fear on that count. Your beauty rivals the stars in the heavens."

"If that is true, you should fall prostate at my feet in complete awe."

"You would be happy if I did just that?"

"My husband tossed me aside." She rubbed her arms against the cold breeze invading the hallway. "Haabeel said I am an old used sandal. How will I survive and save Jazmine and my mother if men do not find me attractive?"

"Let me help." He stepped closer.

"If only you could. But how? Unless you can find me a husband greater than King Herod."

His gaze softened. "We could marry. I am not a prince or ki—"

She covered his mouth. "Stop! You are speaking utter nonsense. Father would never agree. And you know I would hate trading my lovely clothes for plain tunics."

He did not smile at her feeble jest. He gently removed her hand.

"I am speaking utter nonsense. But the thought of you and Herod and..." His face blazed bright red. "I hate it for you."

Flustering men usually delighted and amused. But not now. Not in the face of Avda Hama's genuine care for her well-being.

"You should not have had to witness what you did. I promise to be more discreet."

His jaw tightened. "There has to be another way."

"You cannot save me, Physician Hama. So do not try." She hated to hurt him, but he was not leaving her any choice.

"Kitra, please," he pleaded.

He was breaking her heart. He truly was.

She turned and fled. Her mind reeled as she hurried through a maze of palace hallways. A marriage proposal from Physician Hama. How bizarre. What could he have been thinking? He was a dear man and would make an honorable, courageous champion for a sweet Jewish maiden.

Kitra, however, was the daughter of the ambitious cousin of the king of Nabatea. Her fate had been chosen for her. If her fortunes were to rise, she would need to secure a spectacular marriage. She had given Father a prince for a son-in-law.

If all went according to plan, Father would soon be able to brag that his favorite daughter was the wife of King Herod.

CHAPTER 11

Resisting the urge to follow Kitra, Avda paused outside the wooden door to the secluded chamber Herod used for private meetings.

"Collect yourself, Avda," he lectured himself.

His desire to rebuke Herod for dallying with Kitra had died a painful death with a few crushing words.

You cannot save me. So do not try.

Kitra could not know how deeply the words had cut.

Avda had not been able to save Mary after Benjamin's birth. He had been covered in blood up to his elbows, but none of his training and knowledge of medicine had helped. The terror in her eyes as she bled to death still haunted him.

And then Chaya took her own life. Poisoning herself with a toxic mix of cures, procured from his medicine baskets. *Infernal flames!* He was a highly regarded physician, yet had not been aware Chaya was sad or unhappy.

What made him think he could rescue Kitra?

She clearly did not want his help.

He exhaled heavily.

His responsibility rested with Ori and Benjamin.

He would do well to keep his focus on his sons.

He knocked loudly on the door as a remedy against catching Herod assaulting another young woman.

The red-headed slave Niv showed him into the sparsely furnished room.

Avda halted upon spotting Herod's sister Salome perched vulture-like on the edge of a chair. She had not inherited a speck of her mother's beauty. Her nose was overly sharp. And her mouth hard. But it was the malicious glint in her eyes that unfailingly made Avda's skin crawl. "Physician Hama, it is kind of you to finally join us."

Herod was ensconced behind a substantial wooden desk. He smiled in greeting. "Kitra slapped you, did she? My cousin is quite the feisty temptress."

Avda rubbed at his cheek, hoping the mark faded before Ori or Benjamin or others asked about it. Still aggravated with both Herod and Kitra, he could not wait to escape to the privacy of his chambers. Crushing mixtures of medicines in mortar and pestle was pleasant work.

"You needed my help with a small matter."

"Sit. This may take some time." Salome pointed a bony finger at the empty desk chair next to hers.

Avda's muscles tightened. Though it was never wise to cross Salome, he remained rooted in place, reminding the trouble-making woman that she had no power over him. At the same time, his palms grew hot and clammy. He had not survived all these years of service to Herod, and his father before him, without an eye for trouble.

"I thought this was a small matter."

Salome's features pinched. "We know the queen confides in you. You would not be keeping any secrets from us, would you?"

"I do not act as anyone's confidant. I tend to sicknesses.

If the queen falls ill, you will be the first to know." Avda had no patience for palace intrigues.

Herod leaned forward. His expression clouded, he rested his elbows on his knees. "I fear my wife and her grandfather are hatching a plot against me."

This was nothing more than Salome poisoning her brother's mind against the queen. Once again.

"I do not believe it. I have been treating High Priest Hyrcanus for pain in his joints. He mostly reminisces about the past and tells me stories from his days as High Priest. Sometimes he speaks of his captivity in Parthia. Truthfully, your name never comes up."

Herod nodded, but the storminess did not clear from his eyes. "I am glad to hear it. And I can tell the Herodian haters that John is being well cared for."

"The queen's mother is not feeble-minded," Salome said, her never ceasing criticism of Mariamne and Aalexis was as predictable as it was tiresome.

Ignoring the vulture, Avda met Herod's eyes. "The queen's heart belongs to you. Your distrust pains her."

"She said that?" Herod's tone held a note of both fondness and hopefulness.

Avda smiled with satisfaction. His father used to say, if a physician helped only one person, the day should be counted as a success. "The queen is the mother of your four children. To turn against you is to turn against them."

"Thank you, Avda, for putting my mind at rest. You are one of the few people I trust. You have always been a good friend." His expression cleared, and he straightened, rolling his shoulders.

Friend of the king. It was a title many coveted. Avda loved Herod and had remained loyal, even in light of

Herod's faults, weaknesses, and dubious actions. Did that count as friendship?

Salome glared coldly at Avda. "And as the king's friend, you will be sure to keep a close eye on the queen and her Hasmonean family."

"You are asking me to spy on the queen?" Avda pretended astonishment, when what he felt was disgust for Salome's incessant attempt to ruin Herod's affection for his wife. Salome would be the first to cheer if Kitra replaced Mariamne. Salome might be behind the idea of Kitra seducing Herod.

"Spying is too strong a word." Herod used a cajoling tone, but there was no mistaking he was giving an order rather than making a suggestion. "But be sure to report anything that seems out of the usual."

Salome drummed the desk slowly. "We all know the king rewards his loyal followers." What was left unsaid hung heavily in the air. Those who crossed King Herod received no mercy.

Avda would not bend to the threat. What kind of physician would he be if he put his own well-being above others?

"If we are finished here, I promised your mother I would check on her to see if the new cure is helping with her headaches."

Dismissed by Herod's nod, Avda hauled open the wooden door and escaped down the dark hallway.

Herod's sister had accomplished the opposite of what she wanted.

Avda would do all in his power to save Kitra and Mariamne from falling prey to Salome's latest plot.

CHAPTER 12

Newly arrived at King Herod's winter palace for a visit of indeterminate length, Elizabeth pressed deeper against the cushioned reclining couch and stroked Apollo's sleek black fur.

James burst into the opulent guest chamber. Agitation simmering from him, he strode to her. "Your banquet gown will be covered in cat hair. I told you it would be best to leave the hairy beast behind in Jerusalem."

Apollo's white-tipped ears flattened, and his claws dug into her lap. She held tighter to the cat. "I wish you would learn to ignore his blustering, my darling boy." Not that the ten days since the blasphemous marriage had done anything to ease the tensions between James and her.

He pointed to the door. "The guests are assembling in the banquet hall."

She second-guessed her decision not to send to Galilee for Gabriel. Was it selfish to expect her brother to abandon his wife and two small children and his olive farm to help untangle her raveled affairs?

"Do you really believe a wedding banquet hosted by King Herod will melt the riotous opposition to our sinful marriage?"

James's jaw clenched. "There is nothing sinful about our marriage. You are allowing Jerusalem's pious rabble-rousers to influence you."

"Because the need to make our escape from Jerusalem to Jericho under the cover of darkness was somehow enjoyable. Is that any way to live?"

He knelt beside her and his tone turned gentle. "Be patient. The city will soon find something new to be outraged over. The wedding banquet is a good first step to turning the tide."

Apollo hissed and arched his back.

She drew the cat to her chest. "Shh." The attempt to hush him did not succeed in calming her or Apollo. "James, I beg you to end this. Divorce me."

He stood, towering over her. "We are making progress. You are, at least, viewing the marriage and the marriage contract as valid."

"Accepting this truth does not change anything." She glanced at the plush bed dominating the room.

His eyes turned stormy. "I will sleep on the reclining couch. Unless you would like me to find a bed in the slaves' quarters. Luckily for me, King Herod has many lovely slave girls."

"Do as you like," she said, although misery welled.

"Forgive me. That was cruel."

She pressed her cheek to Apollo's fur. He meowed a complaint at her tight hug. "I can sleep on the reclining couch."

"We can settle this argument later. In the meantime, it is never wise to keep a king waiting." James's frown deepened, but he held out his hand.

Apollo hissed and spit.

"James is the only friend we have." She rubbed his boxy

head. The reminder was for herself as much as Apollo.

The cat bounded from her lap to the bed and prowled around.

Taking a deep breath, she locked eyes with James. "How many people are attending the banquet?"

"Too many." He grunted as though pained. "Actually, Saul and Phaedra will be in attendance. They will offer their blessings on our marriage."

She stood on unsteady legs. "That does not make any sense."

"King Herod insisted. He wants to see your reputation restored."

"The king?"

"I may have made the initial suggestion." He shifted in place. "Saul and Phaedra were wise enough to see the advantage of pleasing the king in this matter."

"I am happy to make peace with them, but not with the whole palace watching."

"A public audience is best."

Anyone with a jot of feelings would recognize it would be difficult enough for her to attend a wedding banquet hosted by the man who had killed her father. Adding Phaedra and Saul to the mix was too much to ask.

"For whom?" she said between clenched teeth.

"I thought you would be pleased."

"Rubbish! This is about you worming your way closer to your goal of being named King Herod's master builder."

His face drained of color, causing the jagged scar to stand out. "I have upset you. What can I do to make amends?"

She rubbed her aching forehead. "You win tonight. But stop using me as a game piece in your war."

"War?"

Heaviness pulled at her soul. Why couldn't he see the truth? "Your father is dead, but you—"

"Do not drag *him* into this."

A chilly blast raced down her spine. "As you please."

He crossed the room and hauled open the door. "Proceed with caution at the banquet. Do not trust anyone or anything. Life is safer that way."

She stared into his black raven-like eyes. "You trust me."

"Do not trust anyone," he repeated and marched away.

Life had to be lonely behind the wall he had erected around his heart. No. She would not be sad for him. She refused to be sad for James Onias.

Considering this was her third marriage and third wedding feast, Elizabeth ought to have mastered the art of smiling when greeted with felicitations for a happy marriage and ignoring the scrutinizing stares, but her insides churned. Time could not have dragged more slowly if she were a criminal on a cross, counting the moments until her life's blood dripped away.

A palace slave serving wine paused at Elizabeth's elbow, and her half-empty goblet soon brimmed with a dark ruby liquid. Gaudily clad guests filled the opulent hall. The air was thick with the smell of roasted meats. Cheers rose from the head table as King Herod roared with laughter and hefted his goblet in another toast.

Her lack of height a frequent frustration, Elizabeth strained for a better look.

Seated on either side of the king, James and Saul laughed with the other men and exchanged a few words.

Her brother Andrew also sat in attendance on the king. He had not looked at her once. Though not a surprise, the rejection hurt.

The mood around Queen Mariamne's table was subdued. The unmarried girls whispered together under the watchful eyes of mothers and chaperons. The queen and her mother Aalexis continued to be tight-lipped

Elizabeth and Mariamne were of a similar age and were both daughters of high priestly families, but she could not recall ever having the opportunity to speak more than two words to the woman. Like her, Mariamne had grown up cloistered at home, visiting the Temple only during the major feasts or making the occasional foray to the upper market.

Aalexis was the matriarch of the Hasmonean family. Hints of her former beauty lingered, despite the many trials she had endured. Witnessing her storied family's fall from power and the unstoppable rise of the savage Herodians. Her daughter's marriage to Herod. Her beloved son's drowning death.

Elizabeth missed her own mother terribly and wished her health would have allowed her to travel down from Galilee. James promised to take her to visit Mother and Gabriel shortly. The prospect of the trip was a lone bright spot.

Queen Mariamne sent a scathing glance toward the latest noisy outburst from the table presided over by Herod's mother. "It is a pity my husband will not hear of sending his extended family back to Idumea."

Aalexis paused from beating the air with her fan. "Nothing good comes of allowing unmarried girls to attend banquets. Your husband will not be happy until Jerusalem is indistinguishable from Alexandria and

Rome."

Elizabeth almost wished she had been seated at the other table. It would have allowed her to hide behind the nonstop chatter and giddy laughter. And afforded her the opportunity to observe James's ex-wife more closely.

Kitra's full red lips, revealing gown, and silver bangles, and her vivacious manner were meant to draw eyes and cause jealousy. James, who was unfailingly harsh in his judgments, never uttered an ill word about Kitra, which only increased Elizabeth's curiosity.

The queen wrinkled her lovely nose. "The king is a great admirer of foreign ways."

Aalexis nibbled on a chunk of mutton. "Next he will insist you and I accompany him to synagogue."

"I have gotten great joy from synagogue," Elizabeth said. "The prayers and singing and reading of the scriptures are uplifting."

Mariamne turned to Elizabeth, showing her first real interest in her presence. "You found Egypt tolerable."

Daily life in Egypt had come as a wonderful surprise. She sighed with longing.

"At first I found the liberty of walking about Alexandria on my own quite dizzying. But I quickly got used to it and a day seldom passed without my venturing somewhere."

Aalexis gasped. "You went out by yourself?"

Her return to Jerusalem meant a return to a life of imprisonment and solitude. The last ten days cooped up inside James's home was torture on more than one level. She managed a sad smile. "A slave always accompanied me."

Aalexis looked down her royal nose. "If Saul Boethus had kept a closer eye on you, you might still be married."

The young women gathered around the marble table giggled.

Queen Mariamne silenced them with a glance, then her cool gaze targeted Elizabeth.

"The king will not hear of sending you and your new husband into exile to Egypt or Italy." Her voice was no less lethal for its softness. "I told him it would be a kindness as your unseemly marriage might find more acceptance among the Jews of Alexandria or Rome."

Elizabeth choked down a sip of wine. She had expected a frosty reception from many in the royal family, but the reprimand still stung. And though she would dearly love to escape back to the life she had grown comfortable with in Egypt, overcoming James's pig-headed obstinacy would be a monumental task.

As if her marriage banquet was not going badly enough, her stomach sank upon spotting Phaedra make a late entrance to the hall.

With her blunt chin-length hair, painted red lips, and white-pleated tunic, Phaedra looked like a hieroglyphic figure come to life. A widow for the fourth time and already in search of a new husband, she was no doubt pleased with the attention on her meandering route to the queen's table.

Aalexis pursed her mouth. "Did you not warn your former husband and sister-in-law that their eccentric ways would be a liability here?"

"It would have been a waste of breath." Elizabeth dug at the pad of her thumb with her fingernail.

"Indeed," the queen replied tightly. "My husband could not be more delighted with Saul and Phaedra's strangeness."

Aalexis glared in the direction of the head table and

strangled the silver fan handle. "Until he is not delighted —and turns on them."

Elizabeth's heart pounded harder, unsure of what kind of reception to expect from Phaedra. They had always been on good terms—until she and her brother had tried to have her killed.

Phaedra glided to a stop, and her hand lighted on Elizabeth's shoulder. "Dear sister-in-law. I hope you are not telling tales about me?"

Elizabeth forced a smile.

Before abandoning Egypt for Israel, Phaedra and Saul had quizzed her about the royal household, probing for an advantage in winning favor with the king. But they also had been trying to determine how many of their secrets she knew. They were especially interested in Cleopatra's agents offering the brother and sister a generous reward if they took part in a plot to poison King Herod. Elizabeth thought she had satisfied them to her ignorance of the matter. But something must have spooked the brother and sister, prompting them to turn on her.

She was still shocked at their willingness to kill her. Had the fondness they showed her been a ruse? Did they know her so little after eight years she lived with them to believe she wished to destroy or hurt them? How could she convince them they had nothing to fear?

She clasped the older woman's hand. "You know I always strive to be discreet."

Phaedra pulled her hand free and primped her black-dyed hair. "Which is more than I can say for my late husband."

The murmur of conversation dimmed, and eager eyes focused on them. Amusement flickered in Queen Mariamne's eyes.

Elizabeth's face heated. Jonah was the last subject she would have broached. She considered offering her sympathies but rejected every formulation of words ricocheting through her mind.

Phaedra circled the table to an open chair. "Let my troubles be a lesson to the young maidens. Think twice before convincing your fathers to arrange a marriage because you are enamored with a man who has beautiful eyes. This was the second time for me, and it did not work out any better than the first."

The young girls tittered, and the older women looked equally amused.

As Phaedra took her seat, Aalexis put her fan to her mouth and spoke a few quiet words in the other woman's ear. Most likely a stern lecture to act with more decorum at the queen's table.

Momentary surprise showed on Phaedra's painted face, followed by a calculating look and a slight nod.

What was that all about? At a guess, something significant.

Angels save her, more trouble was brewing.

"I propose a toast," Phaedra announced brightly.

Her heart in her throat, Elizabeth lifted her cup.

Phaedra's lips curved with a coy smile. "Blessing on your marriage, dear sister-in-law."

"I am pleased we are to be on friendly terms." Elizabeth hoped her jitters did not show on her face.

Phaedra studied her for an uncomfortable long moment. "As am I. Especially if King Herod employs both my brother and your husband to be master builders."

Queen Mariamne did not raise her goblet. "My husband would do better to concern himself with the impending audience before Octavian."

Aalexis waved her gray fan at a trio of slave girls. "Stop gawking and serve up the last course."

The chastised slaves hurried to obey.

The banquet could not end soon enough for Elizabeth. For once she was eager to be alone with James and relate what she had witnessed between Phaedra and Aalexis.

The question was—how much should she reveal? Despite their treachery toward her, she had no desire to see Saul and Phaedra imprisoned or killed. She did not trust James to share her concern. She suspected he would go straight to King Herod with the information regarding their involvement with Cleopatra. And most likely rejoice if the king ordered their execution.

She clutched the wine goblet. Fear of James's reaction churned her insides. But his life and hers might be at risk if she held close to her secrets.

CHAPTER 13

J ames could not help but note the workmanship on display at every turn of the palace hallways. The colorful frescoes, Doric columns, and polished stone floors were exquisite. His envy because he had not been the master builder responsible for this gem of a palace took second place to concern over Elizabeth's pensive silence after their departure from the wedding feast.

His gut was a twisted mess thanks to an afternoon of worrying over her welfare. He followed her into their rooms.

Apollo hissed at James from the safety of the reclining couch.

"Be quiet, you wicked beast," James scolded.

The cat jumped to the floor and sauntered into the next room.

James grasped Libi's elbow before she could likewise escape to the bedchamber.

"What happened? Were the women cruel? Did Phaedra attack you when she finally showed up? If I learn any of them were unkind to you, they will have to deal with me."

"I was *zavah*." She raised her chin. "It made me strong. I

am perfectly capable of defending myself if necessary."

His blood heated at the sight of her fiery black eyes and heart-shaped face. The hint of womanly curves beneath her silky royal-blue gown was too distracting.

"Libi, you were the most beautiful woman at the banquet. I could hardly concentrate as the king quizzed Saul and me on how we would go about construction of a breakwater for a man-made harbor."

"What nonsense. Queen Mariamne's beauty is sheer perfection. And your ex-wife Kitra is stunning. Surely, today's banquet must have brought up memories of your wedding to Kitra?"

He winced. "You have no reason to be jealous of Kitra. When you are present, I am blind to other women."

"James." She covered her ears. "I have something important to tell you, but I will keep the information to myself if you insist on continuing with your foolish rambling."

Tempted to pull her into an embrace and kiss her until they were both panting, he crossed his arms and dredged up a stern look.

"Not telling me all you know could be a fatal mistake."

Her shoulders fell. "First, though it pains me to admit it, you were correct about the wedding banquet. King Herod's blessing swayed opinions. The many felicitations on the marriage and wishes for happiness seemed sincere."

If he was a joyful man, he would be smiling.

"You should be pleased. It means you will be able to move freely around the palace for the rest of our stay here. The same will be true of Jerusalem once you are Queen Mariamne's guest in the Women's Court at the Temple."

Her face clouded. "The queen and her mother are not pleased with Herod, especially his blessing our marriage."

"Shh," he cautioned, glancing over his shoulder as if the walls had ears. "This is a precarious time. Herod is always full of suspicions, but the wait for Octavian's summons has set him more on edge. Our wedding banquet was a short distraction, but I would not be surprised if he is pacing his quarters like a caged lion."

"What will you do...where will you go if the king is deposed?"

"You mean...what will *we* do? Where will *we* go?"

"You will not let me forget *we* are married, will you?"

"No, never." He sounded like a brute to his own ears. He started over again. "Thanks to my father's greed, *we* are fabulously wealthy. If matters go badly for King Herod, *we* can make Rome or Egypt or any number of other cities our new home."

Hope filled her eyes. "We should go anyway. I do not trust the king or Aalexis *or* Phaedra."

"I will not walk away." He crossed his arms.

She poked his chest. "Why not?"

"You think it is because I am as obsessed with ambition as my father. But you are wrong. And I am not bragging when I say I am one of the best master builders of this generation."

"So why are you clinging to Herod?" she demanded. "Surely you can find work elsewhere."

The truth was he did not know of another king with Herod's vision and hunger for building. He searched for an answer that would satisfy her.

"All royal courts are dangerous places. Starting over somewhere else could require five to ten years to prove my talent as a master builder. But King Herod is already comfortable with me and respects my skills."

"I am not going to win this battle, am I?"

He clasped her arms. "Libi, I promise to keep you safe. But I need your help. You must confide in me." She did not push him away. That was a start. "Tell me about this important information you have."

She studied him for a long moment, then massaged her temple. "It is something I saw. I might be making too much of it. Maybe it was all my imagination."

"I trust your instincts. You are the least dramatic person I know."

That earned him a small smile, and she described the brief exchange of Aalexis whispering behind her fan to Phaedra.

The Hasmonean family were traditional rivals of the Onias family, and as such James had no fondness for Aalexis.

"This would not mark the first time Aalexis conspired with foreigners to the detriment of her son-in-law the king."

Elizabeth nodded. "Alexandria was always abuzz with gossip over Cleopatra's attempts to undermine and disgrace King Herod. They say Aalexis and Cleopatra regularly exchanged letters."

"I have heard the same rumors. Aalexis has good reason to feel vulnerable now that Antony and Cleopatra can no longer protect her. Do you have any guess as to why she would turn to Phaedra and Saul?"

She shook her head. "As far as I know they were not acquainted with anyone in King Herod's household before coming to Jerusalem."

"So why would Aalexis reach out to Phaedra?" He pondered the possibilities. "I doubt she is hoping to befriend Saul Boethus's lowly widowed sister. I will poke around, see if the palace slaves have noticed the couple acting oddly. That is to say...more than usual."

Her ivory skin paled. "Promise me you will not go to King Herod unless you find solid evidence against Saul and Phaedra."

He led her to the couch and encouraged her to sit. He knelt. "It sounds as if you trust them more than me."

"They always treated me kindly." She studied her hands.

Her answer did not sit right. He tilted up her chin. "What are you keeping from me?"

"I promised I would never tell."

Fear and jealousy tangled his gut. He worked to keep his voice gentle. "I cannot protect you if you keep secrets from me."

"My marriage to Saul was not a real marriage." Tears glistened in her eyes.

James blinked. "That is not the answer I was expecting. I am not sure what to say."

"When Saul and I married I learned he was in a long-term affair with an older woman who was married."

His mouth dropped open. "A woman, but the way he dresses, I thought—"

"He is guilty of vanity," Libi replied curtly. "He likes the attention that comes with the peculiar clothes and dramatic makeup."

"Tell me more about the affair." James's mind continued to reel. "And why the marriage to you?"

She traced the delicate stitching decorating her gown. "Ruth was the wife of a prominent rabbi. She was twenty years older than Saul. The affair started when he was sixteen and a student living in the rabbi's home."

"Fickle Fortuna," he muttered.

"That was my initial reaction. But it was a love match. Saul was devastated when Ruth died. It has been two years and he still sheds tears over the loss."

"So he married you to hide the affair? I cannot fathom why you tolerated the arrangement." He hated the sadness in her eyes.

"At the time it came as a relief. My father had just been executed. Andrew had to marry King Herod's niece. You —" her voice cracked "—you and Kitra were husband and wife."

He captured her fluttering hands. "The thought of you married to another man, but especially the Egyptian, gutted me. But if your marriage was for show, that means…"

Blushing a deep red, she scrambled off the couch, then whirled on him.

"This is my third marriage and I am still a virgin. That is not something many can boast of."

Blood rushed through his veins like fiery arrows. Holy hellfire. Elizabeth was a virgin. He did not know whether to laugh, or cry, or fall at her knees and beg her to come to his bed.

CHAPTER 14

Elizabeth clapped her hand to her mouth. Heart fluttering like a trapped sparrow, she flew to the bedchamber door, then to the plush bed, then to the round dining table. But there was no escaping James's stare.

What had possessed her to confess she was still a virgin?

She gulped down air. "Do not look at me that way."

"Libi, you have given me a great gift." His voice was thick with emotion. "To be the only man you have ever known."

"Nothing has changed," she said forcefully to hide her embarrassment.

James's black eyes flashed, and he stormed to her. "How can you say that?"

"Do not come any closer." She extended her arms.

He halted, his anger a dark billowing thundercloud. "You should have informed your brothers of the Egyptian's unsavory proposition. They would have interceded on your behalf to end the fraudulent marriage."

The subject was as wince-worthy as the topic of her virginity. She hugged her body, remembering her exhilaration and terror at the prospect of independence after a lifetime of living in seclusion and limited choices.

"Saul and Phaedra promised me unheard-of freedom. I would be free to come and go as I like. Free to spend my dowry as I wished. Free to make my own friends. The first year I went out every day, exploring the markets. I visited innumerable synagogues, attended plays at the theater, sailed on the Nile."

"You went sailing?" James's brows popped higher. "I do not know this adventurous woman you speak of. What did you do with my staid, sensible Libi?"

"It might not have been righteous to turn a blind eye to Saul's adulterous affair. But I would do it again."

"Libi, you have managed to shock me speechless for a second time now."

"Let me finish." She studied her sandals as more memories rolled in. "The first year passed at a dizzying speed. And though the new experiences were marvelous, my heart felt empty. But on my wanderings, I came across a Jewish sect made up of men and women who assist poor widows. I began by offering gifts of food and clothes and coin, but what I cherished most were the rounds of visits that soon filled my days. Tidying houses for those too lame to leave their beds. Feeding those too weak to lift a spoon. Brushing the hair of those too frail to care for themselves."

James's sandal nudged hers. "You have lived a very different life these last nine years from the one I envisioned."

She forced herself to meet his eyes. "I was sick at heart when Saul and Phaedra informed me they were relocating to Jerusalem."

"Why didn't you tell me the truth sooner?" he whispered.

"Does knowing make a difference? Has it changed your mind? Will you heed my request and allow me to return to my ministry in Egypt?"

"There must be poor widows in Jerusalem. Minister to them if that is what gives you joy."

"Now it is my turn to be speechless."

He reached for her hands. "We will send coins and goods to your Egyptian widows." Scars from his stone-cutter days flecked his knuckles.

"That is very good of you, James." She tugged fruit-lessly against his grip. "If you are truly concerned for my happiness and welfare, you will rip up the marriage contract and allow me to live the rest of my days in Egypt."

"What about children?" Sadness flicked across his face. "All women want children. You will be a wonderful mother."

The resurrection of painful regrets weakened her knees. "Of course, I mourn for the children I will never have."

"What kind of talk is that? There is still time for you to bear a child."

"I am a cursed woman." She squeezed her eyes closed.

He caught her to his chest and spoke in her ear. "You are not cursed. That is my father talking."

She reared back. "Simeon Onias is dead. He holds no power over me."

"He was responsible for your exile to Egypt. He arranged your marriage to the Egyptian Saul Boethus. He would rejoice to know he has won."

She pushed against James's chest. "You are wrong! This time, it is my choice to go to Egypt."

He released her and retreated to the door. "No, you are

running away."

"I am not running." The sympathy shining in his eyes galled. "Who are you to accuse me? You hated your father so much, you left your home and family to live with the stonecutters. But that still was not far enough away, so you fled to Rome and studied to be a master builder. And finally, to spite your father, you renounced your priestly duties, your people, and your God."

He grasped the door latch. "I never denied it."

"Where are you going?"

"Libi, I will stop running if you will." A cloud of sadness surrounded him. Then he slipped out the door.

She grabbed a decorative pillow from the reclining couch, threw it, and watched it bounce harmlessly against the floor. "I am not running!"

Exhausted, she slumped down on the couch.

How dare he?

She was not a coward.

Run away? Never.

CHAPTER 15

Moments after ending the fight with Libi and fleeing the bedchamber, James prowled the silent palace hallways in the direction of the dark airless cubicles housing the slaves. Once he hunted down Niv, he would order the red-headed slave to find him a room with a cot and bring him a pitcher of wine and two mugs.

Niv possessed a fountain's worth of palace gossip. A few mugs of wine ought to loosen his lips. If that didn't work, he would revert to extortion. He knew that as a young boy, Niv had played a part in the death of Herod's father. The secret had insured Niv's cooperation in the past. A *friendly* reminder of the debt he owed James for not divulging the secret could not hurt.

Hopefully the slave would provide some useful information, especially in regard to Aalexis and Phaedra. Because brooding over what mischief the sneaky pair were up to was preferable to brooding over Elizabeth.

How long would she resist the marriage? Resist him? How many pitchers of wine would it take to make him stop torturing himself with the fact she was a virgin? And determined to remain so.

The patter of sandals sounded behind him. "James, is that you?"

Recognizing the girlish voice, he groaned and turned back. "Kitra, how have you been? You are looking lovely as ever."

Her tinkling laughter matched the luster in her almond-shaped eyes. "Why are you storming around the palace instead of wooing your wife."

He grimaced. "Is it that obvious I need to do so?"

She sashayed to his side. "There is no need to be a grumpy puppy. The chatter over your marriage has to do with you marrying your stepmother."

"I hate it when you call me that." But he smiled. "You always could see straight through me."

"Poor me," she quipped, then her flirtatious mask evaporated. "I hope you and Elizabeth find peace and happiness."

Touched by her genuine care, he gave her a peck on the cheek. "I am sorry your prince proved a disappointment."

Their marriage had been destined to fail, but the one bright spot was their shared candor. They were always brutally honest with each other, starting with her confession that she had murdered his father at the behest of her father. She had believed James would be pleased. He never blamed her. Like him, she had a father who used her to advance his lust for power and wealth.

"I will marry a king, and all will be well." She toyed with the bangles circling her wrist, then brightened. "I promised my daughter I would take her to the gardens to watch the stars come out. She begged me to invite Physician Hama and his sons."

He was glad to see her high spirits remained intact. "I

wish you well on your search for your king husband."

She kissed his cheek and swept down the hallway. "Getting drunk is not the answer," she called over her shoulder. "Go back to your bedchamber and your wife."

He exhaled and trudged on. He hoped she found true happiness but feared she would remain as restless a soul as him.

He turned down the next hallway and almost collided with the Egyptian and Phaedra. His muscles tightened. "What brings you to this far corner of the palace?"

Saul lifted his goateed chin. "We could ask the same. Are you already bored with your wife and out on the hunt for a slave girl?" He directed a smile at his sister. "When we were students in Rome, James held his own nightly orgies, imbibing to excess in women and strong drink."

"Whereas your affair with the rabbi's wife and tricking a woman into a false marriage were somehow commendable?" The Egyptian's continued trifling regard for Elizabeth boiled James's blood.

Saul's rouged face paled. "My sins arose from love. That is more than you can say. Hate is all you know. Look at you stroking that hideous scar and hating everyone."

"This is not about me. It is about Elizabeth." Ears buzzing, James thrust his fisted hands to his side.

Phaedra clucked her tongue. "You would have thought two Jewish boys schooled among pagans would be natural allies."

"James never fit in," Saul replied in a defensive tone. "He scowled at everyone and boasted that he would build more palaces, fortresses, and grand homes than any of us."

James had been eaten up with hate for his father and making friends was not a goal. He had earned the praise of his tutors, and that was acceptance enough.

"My achievements speak for themselves."

"You build marvelous houses." Saul's smirk was strained. "Houses that fall down. Oh, but that was the foreman's fault, not yours."

James's gut clenched. "The concrete was infer—"

"Bury the past and act like men instead of boys," Phaedra scolded. "We have more important matters to discuss."

Saul plucked at his frilly tunic. "Why do we have to include him?"

"Because we want the same thing. Now invite James Onias to our quarters to share a cup of wine."

It is a mistake to trust him." Saul stalked away.

Phaedra's brow furrowed as she watched him disappear around the next corner. "Ruth doted on him."

"Older sisters have been known to do the same with younger brothers," he remarked.

"I had hoped marriage to a lovely young wife would tempt him away from the old harpy." She sighed. "He will not cause any trouble. I will make sure of that."

If Phaedra believed she could manipulate him as easily as she did her brother, she was in for a rude surprise.

"What is the invitation about?"

She turned shrewd eyes on him. "Something we both want—gaining favor with King Herod."

"But we are rivals."

"Not necessarily." Her smile was as blindingly white as her pleated tunic.

A short while later, James sat perched on the edge of a gilded, cushioned chair opposite Saul and Phaedra in a roomy suite that was easily three times larger than his and Elizabeth's apartment. Ornate brass lamps filled the air with the cloying scent of spikenard oil. Bathwater lapped at the sides of their private pool. All luxuries meant to impress and awe King Herod's most honored guests. It was only natural the brother and sister would be given the larger suite. He should not read too much into it.

After serving wine, a bald slave wearing the costume of a gladiator and an older slave woman dressed like a Roman matron were dismissed. The Egyptian and his sister smiled at him behind their painted faces. How had Elizabeth survived years of this ridiculousness?

Fickle Fortuna, Herod might retain Saul as his master builder for the entertainment value alone.

Though he would like nothing better than to guzzle the goblet of wine clutched in his hands, he needed all his wits in case the meeting was an elaborate trap.

"Explain yourselves. Why am I here?"

His makeup melting from the rigors of the day, Saul leaned forward. "Jerusalem is not—"

Phaedra laid her hand on her brother's arm, but her piercing eyes remained on James.

"Our time in Jerusalem, and now here at the palace has been—shall we say—enlightening." Distaste colored her voice. "Spies abound at every turn in Herod's household. A red-headed slave who seems partial to you has been particularly tiresome."

"Niv has a knack for being irritating."

A hint of a smile showed on Phaedra's red lips. "And our dear observant Elizabeth no doubt noticed Aalexis whispering in my ear."

"The queen's mother excels at stirring up trouble," James growled. "A trait you appear to have in common."

"She asked a *special* favor of me. Apparently, King Herod does not trust her and intercepts all her correspondence. Aalexis hoped we would be so kind as to pass on letters to her friends in Egypt."

James was not in the habit of defending Herod. "Aalexis was under house arrest for conspiring with Cleopatra to see Herod dethroned."

"She did not have anything good to say about her son-in-law," Saul remarked in an amused tone.

If the pair were wise, they would keep their distance from the poisonous conflict. The stakes were high and personal. Aalexis blamed her son-in-law for the death of her only son, while Herod held his Hasmonean in-laws responsible for the deaths of his two older brothers and father.

James feigned boredom. If he became embroiled in the matter and the king learned of it, not being named master builder would be the least of his problems. "Why are you telling me this?"

"King Herod trusts you." Phaedra drummed her painted nails against her silver wine goblet.

"I doubt he trusts anyone aside from his brother Pheroras," James said.

Phaedra inclined her head in agreement. "But he is more likely to take your word over ours if you went to him saying we were meeting in secret with Aalexis. But we are trusting you to see the wisdom in aligning with us."

"We will make it worth your while," Saul added.

"Work with you?" James stared, incredulous, at the pair. "What makes you believe I would agree? Furthermore, I cannot see an advantage in it for you."

"We believe Herod will not only survive his audience

with Octavian and keep his kingdom." Phaedra continued tapping her silver goblet. "But we believe he will do it with the blessing of Rome. It will make him the dominant force in this part of the world."

An eager glint filled Saul's eyes. "Including Egypt."

Phaedra spared an indulgent smile for her brother. "We have not found Jerusalem to our liking. We hope to return to Egypt." She grew somber. "In the meantime, we cannot have you working behind our backs to call into question our loyalty to the king."

"You expect me to believe this pile of dung?"

"We will never be happy here," Phaedra said.

Saul gripped his sister's hand. "Egypt is the place for us."

"But what of the glorious palaces and fortresses and cities King Herod plans to construct? Names and places that will stand for a thousand years."

"Happiness is more important than brick and stone," Saul said.

James's jaw went slack. Elizabeth had a soft spot in her heart for Saul. Could this be the reason? He pushed the unsettling notion aside.

"Libi told me you were stripped of your wealth and lost favor with your patrons."

Phaedra stared into her goblet and swirled the wine. "But all could be reversed with a few words from King Herod."

"I long to visit the garden where Ruth and I used to take our walks," her brother said, stroking his goatee.

Phaedra's age-lined face tightened. "I imagine the king would be inclined to grant our request if we were able to provide him with proof of Aalexis' disloyalty. In the meantime, we do not need you and your spies spoiling matters."

"And why am I trusting you?" Nothing added up. The pair comes to Jerusalem. They accuse Libi of adultery. Claim it was all a mistake. And pretend to be in an alliance with Aalexis so they can return to Egypt?

Saul's smile was grim. "To be rid of us."

"Do we have a deal?" Phaedra purred.

James was mightily tempted, good judgment aside.

CHAPTER 16

E lizabeth woke from a fitful sleep to find her cat crouching and hissing at the dark.

James's black silhouette filled her vision in the semi-dark bedchamber.

Instantly awake, she sat up and corralled Apollo.

"You are wrong about my desire to return to Egypt." Annoyed she sounded defensive, she cleared her throat and started again. "I am not running away. I am pursuing a life of purpose and goodness. And where is the wrong in that?"

He settled on the edge of the bed. His face was haggard and drawn.

Apollo snarled a warning.

"We need to talk."

"We are talking." She petted Apollo in soothing fashion.

That earned a tired smile. "You are too lovely for words."

She made a face. "Be serious."

His breath smelled of wine, but his words were not slurred.

Thank goodness.

Come to think of it, she had yet to see him overindulge in strong drink.

"Saul and Phaedra desire to enter an alliance with me...with us."

"I hope you are jesting."

"I am afraid not." He relayed the details and finished by rolling his shoulders. "I find it difficult to believe Saul is sincere about abandoning the quest to be named master builder of Israel and returning to Alexandria."

"It is the one detail of their story that rings true. I warned the pair that Jerusalem would not suit them." She stroked Apollo's sleek fur.

"The entire country does not suit me," he grumbled. "But Herod's vision for rebuilding the city is an opportunity worth the trouble."

Why couldn't he see that his lust for this prize made him vulnerable to opportunists such as Phaedra and King Herod?

"Please tell me you did not agree to the scheme."

"Not yet. I wanted to consult with you."

"Why would you, when you seldom heed my advice?" she asked peevishly.

"That is not true. I respect your opinions. Besides you have a deep knowledge of the couple's ways."

She did. The time had arrived to inform him that her ex-husband and sister-in-law had plotted with Cleopatra in a scheme involving poisoning King Herod.

She laid out what she knew of the plan. "Cleopatra's untimely death put an end to the plot. Or so I thought."

His frown deepened. "Did they try to involve you?"

"Me?" she asked on a gasp. "I accidentally overheard a secret discussion. I am not a murderer."

"Of course not." His pained look turned grave. "But

others—the king—might think you desired to avenge your father's death."

Unease rippled through her, she hugged Apollo. "Revenge belongs to the Lord."

"Is there anything else I should know?" he asked, his tone gentle.

She hesitated over the next revelation. James would not be happy she had not confided the information before now. "There have been whispers over the suspicious nature of Phaedra's husbands' deaths."

He swore under his breath. "Did the viperous woman consider divorce? How many husbands does this Jonah fellow make?"

She winced. "Five."

"And this did not raise any alarms with you?"

Denying the possibility her sister-in-law was a murderer had not served Elizabeth well. Even now she did not want to believe it. "I had hoped the rumors were simply the work of malicious gossip. Jonah did not seem overly concerned."

"This Jonah was not a man of means or wealth. Did she grow tired of him? And why did she marry him in the first place?"

"Jonah was fifteen years younger than Phaedra, extremely spirited, you might say, but he seemed harmless enough. At first. His immaturity did cause tension between them. I am still in shock over his sudden change in behavior." A shiver went through her as she recalled Jonah attacking her and his subsequent execution.

"Rest assured, I have not forgotten nor forgiven the offenses you suffered." James's jaw clenched and unclenched.

The reply offered no comfort. "Despite everything I

have shared, you still have not ruled out accepting Phaedra's offer. Have you?"

The bed creaked as he shifted closer. Apollo snarled. James stared intently at her.

"I can hold my own against the likes of Phaedra. And it will be easier to keep a closer eye on the pair if they believe we are working with them."

"Stubborn man." She hated to admit the merits of his reasoning. "You were easier to deal with when you were a callow youth. When did you grow brave to the point of recklessness?"

"Whereas your tongue remains sharp as ever."

"Forgive me. That was unkind."

James reached for her and Apollo's sharp claws pierced his skin. He withdrew his hand and sucked on a finger beaded with blood. "Fickle Fortuna, cat! We have to come to an understanding if we are to share the same household."

She set Apollo down on the carpet. "Blame palace life for his foul mood. Apollo does not care for it any more than I do. The backbiting and rivalry and intrigues. Constantly having to guard your words and conversations." The cat strolled away.

"And I am a damnable devil for dragging you into my world. The only excuse I have is that I need you, Libi. You must see that?"

She was disarmed by the twin forces of his sincerity and misery.

James needed her. She feared he was correct. Especially since she was going to give her blessing to their alliance with Phaedra and Saul.

CHAPTER 17

D raped in a fur mantle and the sun warm on her face, Kitra bubbled with anticipation as she reached the end of the pathway leading to a miniature amphitheater. Palace guests and family members swarmed in from various pathways. Laughter and good cheer abounded.

Tension at the winter palace had been steadily growing during the four days since James and Elizabeth's wedding banquet. The promise of fresh air and a humorous performance by a traveling band of actors was a welcome new distraction as the king's fate, and therefore his whole household's fate, continued to hang in the balance.

She paused at the top of the fanned seating area to search for Avda Hama. She had seen nothing of him the past two days.

Taj bumped her arm. "You have the look of a woman seeking out her lover."

Her face heated. Why did her brother always have to taunt? There was no need to be embarrassed. Avda Hama was a friend. She waved to a trio of giggling cousins seated in the women's section at the far end of the stadium.

"And whose wife are you intending to seduce now?"

"Here she comes."

She looked in the direction he pointed. Elizabeth and James Onias had entered the small arena from one of the other garden pathways. Kitra jabbed Taj.

"You would be wasting your time. Plus your ex-brother-in-law is well aware of your adulterous games. James would have your head if you tried getting anywhere near her."

"A difficult challenge makes for half the amusement."

"Stay away from Elizabeth Onias," she warned.

"Have no fear. I am aiming higher."

Afraid to ask, she struck out for the women's section.

He caught her by the elbow. "How do you expect to steal Herod from Mariamne if you tromp around like a cow?"

She turned her gaze to the royal platform. As always, Queen Mariamne was the picture of serene beauty listening to her husband the king, who looked like a man very much in love with his wife. Kitra's stomach pitched. How would she begin to undo the royal marriage?

"You will not fail father a second time," Taj cooed menacingly. "You will not fail Mother and Jazmine. You will not fail me."

How was she supposed to move enticingly on feet that suddenly felt leaden? "Be nice."

"Cheer up. Herod might lose his crown, and possibly his life. And whoever Queen Mariamne marries next would be the new ruler of Israel."

Kitra's breath backed up. She glanced around to be sure no one was close enough to overhear them. "Not her. Please not her." The king had executed his own uncle for merely the suspicion of adulterous motives toward Mariamne. And if Taj dared—

"I am not a fool. I will bide my time."

Her brother was her only ally. And despite his faults and weaknesses, she loved him dearly. She touched his arm. "We will not fail each other."

His head snapped around. For a brief instant his eyes looked as cold as a snake's, but then they warmed. "I look forward with joy to the day you claim your crown as queen. And with your help, Father will see all his children make advantageous marriages." His elegant lips thinned. "Then perhaps he will allow me to divorce my odious wife."

"How is Sabina?" Kitra slowed as they neared the women's seating area. His unhappiness pained her.

"She smells like her dogs." He bristled with resentment. "She has ten of them now. Ten!"

The oldest daughter of the commander of the Nabatean army, Sabina preferred the company of her dogs to people. The childless marriage was a disaster in every aspect, but one. The five-year marriage had made Father and Sabina's father immensely wealthy by deals involving the theft and sale of surplus arms, with Herod's army being the main buyer.

"Give a message to the king." Kitra gave her brother's hand a quick squeeze. His growing impatience could spell disaster. "Tell him I am eager for a private meeting."

Taj nodded his approval, but his eyes remained stormy. "Good. I will arrange it." He strode away in the direction of the royal platform.

The giggly daughter of a distant cousin slid over, making room for Kitra on the cushioned stone bench.

Sick at the prospect of seducing Herod, Kitra put on a dazzling smile and took a seat.

The girl leaned close. "My father's face turns purple whenever I beg him to hire the woman who makes your clothes. He says you dress like a temptress, but I think you are ten times lovelier than Queen Mariamne."

Kitra was not sure whether to laugh or whether to cry.

"How sweet of you."

Mariamne was crowned in refinement and royalty. Her brother and grandfather had been High Priests. She was the mother of a future king.

Whereas Kitra was the daughter of an arms merchant. A twice divorced woman. A practiced seductress.

Queen Kitra.

The notion sounded absurd rather than audacious.

The girl giggled and spoke behind her hand. "Here comes your unseemly ex-husband. Imagine marrying your stepmother?"

James was pointing to the benches holding the queen's female family members.

Elizabeth eyed them nervously.

Kitra stood and waved. The jangle of her bangles revived her spirits. "You are welcome to sit here."

The Hasmonean women were a bunch of cold fish, always looking down their noses at the Herodians and those they deemed beneath them. The invitation was not wholly selfless. It would allow her to indulge her longtime curiosity for the woman James had pined for.

There was a brief disagreement between the pair, with Elizabeth winning the argument. Her smile was warm as she joined Kitra.

"Bless you. I was hoping for the opportunity to meet you."

Elizabeth's lack of conceit was promising. Kitra glanced back at James, who continued to hover nearby.

"Our grumpy puppy does not look happy."
Elizabeth laughed delightedly. "Grumpy puppy?"
Kitra approved. James needed someone with a strong spirit who would challenge him. "He will be annoyed I shared the pet name. For your sake and his, I hope he learns to be happy."

"James says he was a bad husband." Sympathy showed in Elizabeth's eyes.

Kitra seldom reflected on the short-lived marriage. Seventeen when they had married and divorced, she had recovered in spectacular fashion by capturing the attention of Prince Obodas.

"We were both at fault. He drank too much. And I nagged him to death." She sighed. "My father put tremendous pressure on me to convince James to return to his priestly duties and use his name and wealth to reach the highest office. But James would not be manipulated. I admired him for it."

The blunt talk did not fluster Elizabeth. "I see why he thinks highly of you."

"He never stopped loving you." Kitra did not point out that Elizabeth's love for James was equally evident. "At first I resented you, but then I grew envious. I wanted someone to love me as deeply as James loved you. He has put you in a difficult position, but you should forgive him. Love is driving him."

Elizabeth shifted uneasily. "Or obsession."

Kitra had watched King Herod drive himself mad over Queen Mariamne.

"Obsession is destructive. James however would gladly sacrifice his life to prevent you from coming to harm."

"You have given me much to think over," Elizabeth

murmured, drawing inward.

A fanfare of horns announced the beginning of the performance, and a trio of costumed actors pranced across the small stage. Loud clapping resounded.

The late arrival of the king's mother Cypros and sister Salome caused a last moment stir.

Aunt Cypros sat down heavily one row ahead of Kitra and Elizabeth. "Physician Hama is a selfish man," she complained to Salome. "He knows how susceptible I am to earaches."

"His son is close to death." Salome replied. "I am sure your ears are the last thing on his mind."

Dread tightened Kitra's chest. "What is wrong with Avda's son? Is it Ori or Benjamin?"

"It was an accident of some sort." Salome shrugged her bony shoulders.

Aunt Cypros picked at her ear. "How long would it have taken him to clean out the wax?"

"Are you ill?" Elizabeth touched Kitra's arm.

Kitra stood on shaky legs. "Excuse me."

"Sit down," Aunt Cypros ordered irritably. "The play is starting."

Kitra could not remain.

Not until she learned what had happened.

CHAPTER 18

The air in Avda's suite was heavy with the smell of an herbal poultice. Ori moved silent as a ghost as he lit lamps to keep the encroaching dark at bay. Avda's feverish prayers for his son's recovery churned in Kitra's ears.

Forty-eight hours into the bedside vigil, she held Benjamin's hand. The sight of his bruised, swollen eyes broke her heart. Too adventurous for his own good, he had ventured into the royal stables and been kicked in the head by a spooked horse.

Avda stopped rubbing the fringe of his prayer shawl and turned to her. Despair haunted his eyes. "I hoped I would not have to operate, but…" His voice cracked.

Pummeled with fear for Avda and the boy, she felt helpless. She rubbed his back. "You are strong, Avda. You will do what you have to."

A shudder racked his body. "Pray for me, Kitra."

Beseeching gods was not her strength, since she switched religions like seasonal changes of attire depending on the beliefs of her husbands. But she had complete faith in Avda. "Benjamin could not have a better physician. If it was Jazmine, I would want you and only you to attend to her. What would you be doing if this was someone else's child?"

"I would be gathering the necessary instruments and supplies."

"Tell me what we need," Ori said, joining them. He squeezed his father's shoulder.

"I have done the procedure one other time. The kit of tools we will need is on the top shelf of the—"

"Father," a faint voice interrupted. Benjamin's bruised eyelids fluttered open. "My head hurts."

"Hallelujah!" Avda kissed the boy's hand. "Praise you, Lord. Praise you."

Ori relinquished his somber composure for a toothy smile. "Welcome back, troublemaker." He tugged his brother's toe playfully. "It is a good thing you have a thick skull."

Benjamin's parched lips ticked upward. "As thick as the physician's scrolls you like to study."

"Ori will prepare some medicine for the pain." Avda's face beamed with love and pride.

Ori winked. "Do you want the potion that tastes like donkey dung or the one that tastes like rotten turnips?"

Benjamin scrunched his nose and winced. "Could I have honey water first?"

"How about if we start with a cloth dipped in honey water to wet your tongue?" Avda touched the back of his hand to Benjamin's brow.

The boy frowned. "I am not a baby."

"You were supposed to be writing and drawing a paper on the phases of the moon." A large dollop of love softened the voice giving the reprimand. "Instead of sneaking off to the stables."

His son's eyes drifted closed. He reopened them, and

his gaze shifted to Kitra. "You are crying."

Kitra wiped her wet cheek and managed a weak laugh. "They are good tears. I am happy you are awake."

"I am sorry for worrying everyone." Guilt flooded his young face. "I am sorry for disobeying you, Father."

"You are well," Avda said. "That is what most matters."

Feeling the intruder on an intimate family moment, Kitra stood. "I will go tell Jazmine you are better. She has been very worried."

Avda clasped her hand. Admiration and something more shined in his eyes. "I will not forget your kindness to us."

Unnerved, she pulled free, and hurried to the door. Why be flustered? Physician Hama was too practical and respectable to be in danger of falling in love with her.

"I was happy to help a friend."

A shadow crossed his face. "Goodnight, friend."

Stepping out into the hallway she welcomed the blast of chilled air on her heated cheeks.

A hand grasped her elbow and spun her around.

"Taj?" she gasped. "You gave me a terrible fright."

A scowl marred his handsome face. "Me? Your hair and dress look rumpled as an old bed sheet."

She tucked a limp strand of hair behind her ear. "I could not tear myself away from the boy's bedside. He is awake and is doing well."

"You are devoting too much time to Avda Hama."

"His son almost died," she snapped back.

"Your priorities rest elsewhere."

The rebuke rippled through her unsettlingly. "I know my duty," she said for her sake as much as his. "Now that the boy is out of danger I will direct all my attention to King Herod."

◆ ◆ ◆

Come morning Kitra had not been able to resist Jazmine's pleas to visit Benjamin Hama. Jazmine adored both of Avda's sons, and they doted on her. Kitra was secretly glad for an excuse to check on the injured boy. He was all smiles as Jazmine quizzed him about his accident, asking questions typical of a four-year-old. The size of the horse proved of particular interest.

At Kitra's insistence, Avda was off checking on his other patients. Aunt Cypros would keep him busy for an hour with her latest complaint of wax in her ears. Kitra would leave immediately upon his return without breaking her promise to keep her distance from Physician Hama.

Why did the resolve sadden her so? And why had the memory of his loving stare occupied her last thoughts before falling asleep and her first thoughts upon waking?

She and Avda had nothing in common. They came from different worlds.

Jazmine was the picture of a princess with her ribbon-laced hair and jewel-studded tunic as she idly fiddled with the silver bangles circling Kitra's wrist. She and her daughter looked as out of place in the Hamas' cozy apartment as palace peacocks plunked down among passenger pigeons.

So why did she always regret the end of her visits?

The simple rooms should hold no appeal. The main decor featured jar-lined shelves and cubbyholes stuffed with scrolls. Odd verdant smells arose as Ori labored over mortar and pestle. Avda's fringed prayer shawl draped a sturdy brown couch.

The only sign of a woman's touch was a pink alabaster vase choked with dried roses. Perhaps she should play matchmaker for Avda. Irritation flared at the image of Avda's marriage to a sweet Jewish maiden. And how selfish did that make her?

Jazmine tugged on her arm. "Mama, what's wrong?"

"Nothing, dearest." She hugged her daughter, taking comfort in youth's bright-eyed innocence.

She needed to focus all her attention on Herod and center her thoughts on Father's joy and triumph if she captured a king for a husband. Failure meant exile to a drab fortress on the Salt Sea.

Avda Hama was not her destiny.

The wrenching sadness of this truth burrowed deep into her soul.

CHAPTER 19

Called away from his son's bedside, Avda stalked through the opulent palace bathhouse. Kitra had kindly stayed with Benjamin earlier in the day, so he could see to his work. Though Ori was capable of keeping a close eye on his brother, Avda would have preferred to remain in his apartment.

Assaulted with the thick air created by the elaborate heating system, his gut revolted upon spotting Salome seated at a small round table beside the tiled pool. Perched on the edge of a hard-backed chair, she eyed him as though sizing up a wounded rabbit.

Household slaves hovered in the background, ready to replenish or remove the plates of fruits, nuts, and cakes.

Herod wrapped his damp robe tighter around him. Water droplets clung to his hair. His black eyes flashed. "Hama, I trust you would have said something if you noticed my wife acting in a suspicious manner."

"I last saw Queen Mariamne several days ago. I did not observe anything amiss." Avda halted at the pool's edge.

Salome pointed a talon-like finger. "Did the adulterous vixen or her power-hungry mother ask you to smuggle letters out of the palace?"

"I am a physician, not a courier," Avda said, temper flaring. As much as he disliked Salome, he respected her fierce loyalty to her brother.

Avda shifted his attention to Herod. Something significant had transpired while he was attending to Benjamin? But what?

"The queen would never betray you. I would bet my life on it."

Herod's jaw clenched. "The truth will be revealed shortly."

"If the queen is acting skittish, she is in good company." These spells of implacable jealousy and grave distrust of Mariamne on Herod's part pained Avda.

"Be sure to report to me if you see anything unusual," Herod ordered, then his gaze softened. "How is your son?"

Avda rolled his tense shoulders. "He is bored and is asking to resume his schoolwork."

Herod chuckled. "That is a good sign."

He returned the smile. "Especially since Benjamin dislikes school as much as you did."

"Waiting for my fate to be decided has me in a foul mood," Herod said.

This was the closest to an apology Avda would get.

"Have you had any news from Rome?"

Herod plucked a grape from his plate and pitched it in the pool. "Nothing official. My sources tell me Octavian is making ready to travel to Rhodes."

"Octavian will see the sense in retaining a proven man," Salome said.

"Or he could call for my head to be lopped off my shoulders." Herod pitched another grape.

Salome's face pinched. A fall from grace for the king

meant disaster for the Herodians. "Do not tempt bad luck by speaking so."

Avda met Herod's stormy stare. As a longtime ally, friend, and physician to the family his fate was wrapped up tightly with Herod's. He trusted Herod. Trusted him with his life. And his sons' lives.

"Your father and mine told me many times you were destined for greatness. They believed it. I believe it."

"Flatterer," Herod growled, but he looked pleased.

"Shall I start calling you Herod the Great?" a strong voice boomed. Faakhir Aretas strolled through the bath's arched entryway accompanied by Taj and Kitra. Her sheer dress, red-painted lips, and seductive perfume would put her in good company with harlots.

Avda's insides iced. He loathed her family for using Kitra as bait.

She paled and slowed.

Her father and brother propelled her forward.

Taj's oily smile sparkled brighter than the pool water. "Kitra spent the whole afternoon primping after receiving an invitation from her cousin the king."

"A visit from Kitra is always delightful," Salome gushed. "I am sure she will find many ways to please and entertain you, Brother."

Avda ground his teeth. Kitra could not have been more supportive or thoughtful during his recent trial, sitting hour after hour with him at Benjamin's bedside. She had a loving heart. But her uncaring father and brother saw her only as a means to greater fortunes.

"Kitra does not look happy with us, Avda," Herod said, his tone amused.

Kitra's blush deepened. She avoided Avda's eyes. "Spending time with my cousin is pure pleasure."

Avda should not interfere. But for the love of all that was good, how was he supposed to sit back and do nothing?

"How is Jazmine's knee? Ori feels horrible about her tripping over his sandals."

Taj grasped Kitra's arm. "You said Jazmine skinned her knee during a walk in the garden."

She tugged free and stepped closer to Herod. "Enough of this boring talk. Shall we soak our feet in the pool, dear King?"

Herod popped a grape into his mouth and directed a smirk at Avda. "Should we ask Avda to join us?"

Salome hopped to her feet. "Physician Hama needs to attend to Mother."

Faakhir—who up to this point had paid no more attention to Avda than the furniture or the slaves—focused on him like a bug to be squashed underfoot. "And you would be..."

"Nobody important." Avda could kick himself for making a mess of the matter.

Herod sobered. "Avda Hama is an old family friend and a trusted physician."

Kitra's tinkling but nervous laugh bounced off the chamber walls.

"Avda, you should not keep Aunt Cypros waiting," she said.

"Avda?" Taj gave Kitra a shake. "Since when are you on such intimate terms?"

Kitra grimaced and swallowed. "We are friends."

"Leave her alone," Avda snarled and closed on Taj.

"Kitra's welfare is no concern of yours." The young man's chest puffed beneath his costly silk tunic.

"Avda, please go," Kitra pleaded, stepping between him

and her brother.

"If you hurt her, I will run a sword through you."

Herod threw his arm around Avda's shoulder and gave a thumbs-up signal. "Such passion, Avda. I will happily lend you my sword if need be."

"Taj," Faakhir barked. "We are done here. Take your sister and go."

Saluting Avda with a rude gesture, Taj herded Kitra toward the arched entryway.

I am sorry, she mouthed with a pained look. The belt of her gauzy gown fluttered around her as Taj whisked her away.

Avda turned to the father. "Kitra has not done any wrong."

"If you value your life, you will stay away from my daughter." Faakhir's eyes were cold as stone.

"You have my word of honor," Avda agreed, intent on securing Kitra's well-being.

Faakhir gave a tight nod of his head and strode away.

Avda might as well have been run through by a sword. The promise to avoid Kitra hurt that much.

Salome glared down her beak. "Explain yourself, Physician Hama."

He directed his answer to Herod. "Kitra was kind during Benjamin's crisis. There is nothing more to it."

"I believe you." Herod arched a brow. "The trouble is, you have the look of a love-struck man."

Avda scrubbed his face. Infernal flames, he was in love with Kitra. How had that happened? And what, if anything, would he do about it?

CHAPTER 20

Kitra waited in the narrow confines of one of the palace's ritual baths as the midnight hour came and went. Lamplight danced over gray walls painted with a white lattice motif. The scent of olive oil teased her nose. She started at a trickling noise interrupting the silence.

She clutched a hand to her chest. Waiting had never been her strength.

Would Avda meet her in secret? After the disastrous clash with Father and Taj the day before, the prudent path would be to stay far away from her. Avda was the wisest man she knew. She should return to her chamber and put him out of her mind.

The door cracked open. "Kitra?"

Relief washed through her. What she needed to say was too important and too complicated to entrust in a letter.

"I had to see you." She clasped his wide hand and drew him deeper into the chamber.

His square-jawed face was lined with tension. "If your father finds out we—"

"I took great care. Jazmine is spending the night with an older cousin. And several of my silver bangles now belong to the red-headed slave Niv in return for delivering the message to you and his promise of silence."

"Niv was a good choice." He glanced around and scowled. "Please tell me you have not used this chamber to meet with other men."

Given that in the past he had caught her seducing men in secluded corners, the question was fair. But hurt welled anyway. "I did not call you here so I could play the harlot."

"Did you ever stop to think I might be jealous?"

Avda Hama. Jealous for her sake? The man who could be counted upon to be levelheaded and calm amid the constant upheaval of palace life? A learned man and skilled physician who was respected by all who knew him? A family man who was raising two fine boys?

What would it be like to be cherished and cared for by a good and honorable man? *What nonsense was this?* She and Avda had no future. He did not possess any of the qualities necessary in a husband. He was not wealthy, or titled, or famed. Regret stabbed her throat like a blade.

"That is a lovely compliment. But you are mistaken."

He moved closer. Many men had lusted after her, but no one had ever looked at her the way Avda did.

"Mistaken?"

"You only think you are jealous." Suddenly shy, she studied her sandals. "You are lonely. You need a wife. A good, respectable wife."

He tipped up her chin. Strong emotion shone in his eyes. "You have a good heart. You are a loving mother. You have great strength and—"

The words of admiration stung at her conscience. She pushed his hand aside.

"A few hours of sitting at an injured child's bedside

does not change who I am and who you are."

His visage darkened. "Who are you, Kitra?"

"I am the daughter of an ambitious Nabatean ruler, an idol worshiper foolish enough to believe I could outshine a beautiful and beloved Jewish queen."

Something resembling love glowed in his eyes. "Your sparkling liveliness and exotic beauty light up every room you enter. It is not your fault King Herod is consumed with love of the queen."

She adored him for his heartfelt adoration and loyalty. But he had missed the point.

"You cannot tell me, that as a faithful Jew, you would have been pleased to see me made queen."

He stared for a torturously long moment. "Herod would have insisted you give up your idols. Just as you did when you wed James. That must have been difficult."

"You know me...I am a butterfly flitting from pretty flower to pretty flower," she said in a dismissive tone, but winced inwardly at the unflattering truth. "First James, then my Nabatean prince, then King Herod. If my father desires a Roman nobleman for a son-in-law, I will give up my idols for Roman gods."

His brown eyes could not have been kinder. "Your life has not been easy."

The last thing she wanted was for him to be sad on her account. She put on a bright smile and jangled her bracelets.

"I have high hopes for my next husband."

But he did not smile or laugh. "May I..." His voice grew rough. "May I kiss you?"

"I could not have heard right."

"Just one kiss." He stepped closer.

Dizzy as if standing at the edge of a cliff, she stared

longingly at his firm mouth. An immediate antidote was needed to put a halt to this madness.

"I helped murder Simeon Onias," she said.

"The whole palace suspected as much." His voice showed no sign of distress. His fingers trailed over her hand.

Heat prickled up her arm. "The snake that bit my father-in-law did not end up inside the lining of the robe by accident."

"But the idea was not yours." He drew her hand to his mouth and kissed her knuckles.

Seventeen and newly married to James and frightened of failing her father, her sole focus had been playing her part to perfection. It was only after Simeon's death that the impact of what she had done hit her with full force. Sick at heart and ashamed, she forced herself to look Avda in the eye.

"I should have sought James's help or refused to give the deadly gift to Simeon."

"James was too self-absorbed to be of help to anybody." He lifted her other hand to his mouth and kissed it.

"You are too kind and good to me." Tears swam in her eyes. She pressed closer.

His hands stroked her sides. "You have never had a man cherish you. You should be cherished."

She was undone. Who would have guessed words of love would hold more value than a chest of jewels or a vast kingdom?

"I wish…" What did she wish for?

Avda's mouth skimmed her jaw. "Kiss me, Kitra."

Her thoughts dissolved. She rose on her toes and kissed him lightly on the lips. He tasted of nuts and salt and wine. Her insides heating, she deepened the kiss. He kissed her back, and their murmurs echoed off the confines of the marble bath walls.

Trembling, she broke off the kiss. Time was running out. And much needed to be said. "Whatever this is, it cannot happen again."

His smile did not diminish the heat and passion in his eyes. "Of course not."

How could she stay away from him? From this? She buried her hands in his thick brown hair and kissed him greedily. Then pushed free. She fanned her face. The tinkling of her bangles was a reproach in her ears.

"I wanted and needed to say a final farewell, but it was not fair of me to ask for the meeting and to draw you into more danger. I cannot bear to think of harm coming to you or your sons."

Pain now etched his handsome face. "The blame would be all mine. I threatened your brother's life and gave him reason to suspect us of improper behavior. I will never forgive myself if I am the cause of your father sending you and Jazmine away or punishing you in any fashion."

"All is well," she assured him. "I explained to Father that you were smitten with me through no encouragement on my part. And that you simply got carried away. Next time slur your words. And I can tell him you are drunk."

A bark of laughter gave way to a groan. "Woman, I am drunk. Drunk on you."

"I never thought I would regret my power to seduce a man."

He arched an eyebrow. "In truth, I seduced you."

She opened her mouth to argue but ended by smiling.

This was a side of Avda she had never seen. She found it highly appealing.

The sound of cheerful voices came from the hallway and faded away. The danger of discovery grew with each moment they lingered. Tempted to kiss him again, she took a step backward.

"From now on we must strive to avoid each other. Promise me you will do all to stay safe. No matter my fate."

"If your father or brother do you harm or—"

Her feelings for Avda and his feelings for her presented the greater danger. "I can take care of myself."

"How? By throwing yourself at the next prospective prince or rich man. By playing the part of a seductress." His features twisted in a scowl.

"I have no choice," she cried. "As soon as my step-mother and half-sisters learned I failed to hook King Herod, they harped at Father, demanding he send me into exile. Rotting away by the Salt Sea is a fate I cannot accept. Plus I have Jazmine's future to think of."

"I beg you to find another way."

The cooling air sent shivers through her. She hugged her body. Seduction was her only weapon. But that is not what he wanted to hear.

"I am eager for suggestions."

"If your father tries to send you away, we will ask the king to intercede. Herod owes me a favor or two."

"It is too dangerous. You should not—"

He squeezed her hands. "Trust me. I will be careful."

Never trust a man. That is what her mother would say. But Avda would not fail her. She nodded and offered him a shaky smile.

"It is getting late."

"We should leave the chamber separately."

Spurred by the same impulse they shared a frenzied kiss.

She left first. The racing of her heart matched the patter of her sandals as she fled down the hall. Avda had not offered any suggestion to the most pressing problem—her need to make a dazzling marriage.

"Vexing man," she whispered.

Why did his kisses have to be so intoxicating?

CHAPTER 21

Exiting the ritual bath moments after Kitra's departure, Avda set off on a roundabout journey through the dark palace hallways in hopes of cooling a volcano of emotions.

Holy Jehoshaphat, what had just happened? He reeled at the memory of Kitra's generous curves and impassioned kisses. He lifted his arm to his nose and inhaled her perfume.

It had taken all his willpower to keep from begging for more than a few stolen kisses. Her words echoed louder. *Whatever this is, it cannot happen again. You are lonely. You need a wife. A good respectable wife.*

As an idol worshiper and murderess, Kitra did not come close to qualifying.

If he was merely suffering from attraction—and make no mistake, he was afflicted with a serious case of desire —he would make a point of steering clear.

But he could not put the idea of *them* away.

His heart was involved.

And not just a little.

After the loss of Mary and Chaya, he had closed his heart, unable to bear the thought of loving and losing a third wife.

What was it about Kitra that made him willing to risk more hurt? And why wasn't he more troubled by the part she had played in Simeon Onias's death?

In the weeks that had followed Simeon's murder the palace had been rife with speculation over what the hateful man had done to provoke Faakhir and a morbid fascination with the snake sewed into the lining of Simeon's robe. Kitra's part in the assassination was mentioned as an afterthought or completely ignored.

When he looked at Kitra he did not see a murderer. No. He saw a brave young woman.

Her belief that her worth began and ended with her beauty and allure pained him.

She had so much more to offer. Ori and Benjamin always brightened when she visited and praised their talents and took delight in their stories. She was raising a spirited, inquisitive daughter. She was an expert at maneuvering the many intrigues and pitfalls of palace life. She was a survivor, not buckling when her husband divorced her and disowned Jazmine. The more time he spent with Kitra the more he found to admire.

Would her next husband bother to look beneath the surface? Not if her father's method of procuring a husband followed past examples. He clenched his hands into fists. Faakhir's unconscionable prostituting of his daughter to increase his riches was beyond sickening.

Avda had begged her to find another way. Despite the considerable distraction of the heated kisses they had shared, he had not lost sight of the fact that she failed to make any promises.

Infernal flames! He detested the thought of Kitra married to another man.

He rounded a corner and slowed. Darkness loomed. The slave responsible for lighting and caring for the hallway lamps had neglected his duty. The fastidious head steward would not be pleased. Not that Avda would report the lapse.

Far down the corridor light escaped from under the double doors to Queen Mariamne's private suite.

He tensed and moved forward. The queen usually retired early.

His ears pricked at the sound of low conversation in the room.

He hesitated at the door, hand poised to knock. It would be embarrassing and awkward if he interrupted the king paying a late-night visit to his wife. If the queen or one of the children were unwell, she would have sent for Avda. But he had been absent from his rooms.

The door creaked open and he and Niv both jumped in surprise.

Niv's freckled face paled, and the young slave looked behind him. "It is only Physician Hama."

The queen, her mother, and her grandfather were gathered around a reclining couch bearing several travel chests. Trepidation and guilt lined their faces. A pair of slaves hovered with clothes and toiletries in hand.

Alarmed, Avda slipped past Niv. The memory of the poolside interrogation by Herod and Salome hit with a wallop. Questions regarding Queen Mariamne acting suspiciously and the keeping of secrets and smuggled letters. "What is this about?"

"Physician Hama, you should not be here," the queen said, her voice strained.

Aalexis swished her gray-plumed fan beneath her chin. "My father is making his escape from the country before the king can execute him."

Herod would be livid. Avda glanced at John Hyrcanus. The old man looked even more haggard than usual. "Escape where?"

The fan beat faster. "The king of Nabatea is sending horses to the border to meet my father and offer him sanctuary."

The news kept getting worse. Herod had just fought a war with the Nabateans. Aalexis was allowing her hatred of Herod to cloud her good sense.

"Herod will consider this treason," he said to John.

Hyrcanus tottered to a nearby chair and collapsed onto a plush cushion. "I desire to live out my life in peace. Is that too much to ask?"

Mariamne knelt beside her grandfather and patted his brown-spotted hand. "It is not too late to change your mind."

Aalexis' posture stiffened. "Daughter, we have discussed this to death. Your husband will not rest until he kills every last one of us."

"His sons carry Hasmonean blood." Mariamne stood and huffed in exasperation.

"See if he does not turn on *them*," Aalexis said. "You should take your children and join your grandfather. Nabatea is the safest place for you."

Avda loved and respected the queen, but her malcontent of a mother was another matter. He narrowed his eyes at the conniving woman. "And how did it work out when you attempted to flee to Egypt with your son?"

Aalexis had the good sense to look embarrassed. Her plan had involved using two coffins to smuggle her way out of the country. Herod had learned of it and caught her in the act.

"I was practically a hostage," she replied, "confined to the palace day and night. The slaves and guards reported my every move to my son-in-law."

Avda examined the prayer shawl packed in the larger travel box and fingered one of the gold-threaded tassels. He could not feel sorry for Aalexis. She, of all people, should not be surprised she remained under house arrest.

"You despised and conspired against the king from the start. Your attempt to deliver your son to Cleopatra proved his distrust was not displaced."

She laughed scornfully. "Unlike my barbarian son-in-law, Queen Cleopatra was true royalty."

Avda's hackles rose. "Herod earned his kingdom by driving an invading army from the country. Your father would still be a prisoner in Parthia if not for Herod."

Her son's death was a festering wound. Anger and hatred oozed from Aalexis' depths. "My son would still be alive if not for your *dearest* king."

Ori was the same age the boy had been upon his death five years ago. So young. So full of promise.

"The drowning was an accident," he said gently. "I saw no evidence in my examination to suggest otherwise."

"Am I supposed to believe you, one of his pet creatures?" She gripped her feathered fan with both hands.

He winced. "I would have left the king's service if I thought him responsible."

Mariamne looped her arm with her mother's. "My husband was terribly jealous of my brother."

Avda had endured more than one sleepless night over the tragedy. Would the boy still be alive if Aalexis and Mariamne had not pushed Herod to make the boy High Priest? The adulation the people had showered on the handsome youth had unsettled the king. But Avda could not believe his friend would stoop so low as to murder an innocent youth.

He shifted uncomfortably. "I wish there was something I could say that would help."

Aalexis pierced him with a scathing look. "Save your pity for yourself."

"Physician Hama, you should go," Mariamne urged. "You are putting your life in danger by staying."

"Yes, run to the king." Aalexis pointed her fan at the door. "I am sure you cannot wait to report our secret."

Duty demanded he report what he had discovered, but it was the last thing in the world he wanted to do. He fell to one knee before Mariamne. "I serve both you and the king. I will not betray you, but you have to promise to abort this dangerous plan."

Mariamne glanced at her grandfather. He had nodded off. She turned her troubled eyes back on Avda.

"My husband is making the same frightening and ridiculous accusations against my grandfather as he did against my brother. We have to get him to safety."

Avda scoured his mind for an answer. The palace was alive with irrational conjecture and fears. How to earn their trust? He cleared his throat.

"Have you considered how difficult the journey to Nabatea will be on—"

The chamber door burst open and guards flooded in.

John Hyrcanus came awake. "Is it time to leave?"

Herod darkened the doorway. "You are not going anywhere, old man. You are hereby arrested as a traitor."

Shaking and pale, John rose. "The king of Nabatea offered to send me four horses as a gift. Where is the crime in that?"

Herod held up several unsealed letters. "Your slave

wisely came to me with your first message."

Mariamne and Aalexis hurried to John and clung to his frail arms.

"Have mercy." Tears streamed down Mariamne's face.

The king's eyes remained wintry. "Did your grandfather intervene when my father was poisoned? Did your cousin Hasmond have mercy on my brother Phasael when he took him prisoner and murdered him? Did Hasmond's army show mercy on my brother Joseph when they slaughtered him?"

Though many years had passed, Herod's grief and fury over the deaths of his father and brothers remained painful and real. The blood feud between the two families had poisoned his and Mariamne's marriage from the beginning.

Weary and sad and feeling all of his forty-two years, Avda stepped forward. "The cold cellar chambers will kill John before he can be tried. Allow him to remain under arrest in his room."

Herod surveyed Avda with a harsh eye. "I did not expect to find you here."

Standing among the travel boxes, Avda felt his mouth go dry. He had all the appearance of a co-conspirator. Was there any denial he could offer that would not incriminate the queen and John? Delay might not help, but it couldn't hurt. "May I suggest—"

"Go back to your boys." Herod's voice was eerily calm.

Feet rooted in place, Avda glanced at John and the women.

"Heed the king, Physician Hama," John said, his expression weary.

Herod signaled for the guards to escort the elderly High Priest out of the room. "Supply him with warm foods, drink, and blankets. We do not want to displease Avda."

The begrudging concession was a small victory given Herod's stubbornness, one Avda would have to be happy with. For tonight.

CHAPTER 22

Several hours later, Avda woke with a start at the urgent knocking on the apartment door. Still fully clothed, he sprang off the reclining couch and yanked the door open.

Lamplight shadowed Niv's distraught face.

A crushing weight filled Avda's chest. He knew the truth without being told. "High Priest Hyrcanus is dead."

Niv nodded and swallowed. "King Herod requests a word with you."

"Give me a moment." Avda made his way blindly towards the bedchamber his sons shared.

Herod had done it. Put to death one of the Lord's priests. One who had ruled many years as High Priest.

Shame washed through him. How many times had he made excuses for Herod's excesses? He had pointed to youthful indiscretion when Herod was put on trial for the death of a zealot, then marched an army on Jerusalem. He had blamed the ugliness of war when Herod executed forty-five revered rulers of Israel. And he had closed his ears to the talk Herod had assassinated Mariamne's young brother.

He had held high hopes Herod would use his many talents to be a great king. But the murder of a harmless old man could not be explained away. Truly great men had compassion and mercy on the weak and vulnerable.

He opened the bedchamber door a crack. Ori and Benjamin slumbered peacefully. As members of the king's household, they enjoyed the best tutors, the finest food, the costliest clothes. The luxuries came at the expense of loyalty to Herod.

He could ignore the murder of a high priest.

Or he could walk away.

His stomach churned at his poor choices.

Escaping Herod's tentacles would not be easy or without sacrifice.

Could he give it all up? Could he leave Herod's service, leave the country, leave his old life behind for a new one? Would his sons thank him for dragging them off to Egypt, Greece, or Rome? What would they think if he stayed?

"Physician Hama," Niv called in a low voice.

Avda pulled the bedchamber door silently closed, followed the slave, and steeled himself to confront Herod.

Niv was unusually silent as they walked through the columned hallway decorated with man-sized urns, then another lined with giant golden candelabras. Their footsteps echoed off the fresco-adorned walls of the gilded throne room. Herod loved to hear praise of his lavish reconstruction of the winter palace. In the light of John Hyrcanus's murder, the beauty was forever tarnished. And Avda's former pride turned to shame.

Reaching the far side of the hall, the slave eschewed the corridor leading to Herod's private chambers for a narrow stairway descending into the bowels of the palace.

Niv did not exchange greetings with the other slaves on the journey through the warren of poorly lit corridors, meanly appointed sleeping cubicles, and large working areas. And they were equally tight-lipped. For good reason. Everyone knew the basement of the royal palace in Jerusalem contained torture chambers reserved to obtain confessions or information from spies and criminals and slaves. No one was safe until the king's killing mood passed.

Avda's step faltered. No. Herod would never put him to torture.

Get hold of your thoughts, he lectured himself. He would learn soon enough the reason he had been summoned.

"You will find him just ahead." Niv halted and pointed, then hurried away.

The king's deep voice spilled from a chamber at the end of the hallway.

Avda's muscles tightened. He forced his feet forward. He would not be cowed by Herod.

A jagged crack inflicted by last year's powerful quake marred the chamber's door frame. He took a deep breath and entered the low-ceilinged room.

Herod and his brother Pheroras stood next to a plain wooden table holding a heavy cord wrapped in a soft cloth. The stink of voided intestines was overlaid with the pungent odor of the liniment Avda used to treat bad knees. Ori had made up a new jar of the medicine earlier in the week for John Hyrcanus.

Herod had the decency to wear a somber face. "He went quickly."

Strangulation was considered the easiest death, and, with the cloth-covered cord, had the added advantage of leaving no marks, but the small mercy could not make up for the fact John had met his end alone in a dark pit instead of in his bed, surrounded by his family.

Avda's hand curled with the urge to punch someone or something. "How could you?"

Pheroras retreated to the filthy cot situated at the rear of the airless chamber.

Herod's mouth thinned. "Let it go."

"Damnation! No. I will not look the other way." Nothing Herod could say or promise would win back his loyalty.

"I did not call you here to be lectured."

"Why am I here?"

Herod's expression was pained. "I am glad for your passion, friend. I feared you might not regain your spirit."

"Do not speak of Chaya or pretend to care." He refused to be swayed by the true concern reflected in Herod's voice. "Not after your treachery toward John...another supposed friend."

Herod studied him for a long moment. "I am off for Rhodes immediately. I have a favor to ask."

"The summons from Octavian finally arrived?"

Herod replied with a tight nod. "Pheroras will have charge over Jerusalem. My mother and sister will proceed immediately to Masada for safekeeping. And Mariamne, Aalexis, and my sons will go to Fortress Alexandrium."

Separating the constantly quarreling women was a wise decision. The solitude of Masada would give Avda room to plan his next move. "No matter the argument between us, I will take good care of your family."

Herod stalked to the door. "You will not be going to Masada. You are to accompany Mariamne. It is my wife's special request."

Avda's pulse jumped. Attending to Mariamne in Herod's absence could be deadly dangerous as Herod's uncle had learned four years earlier, in a similar situation, at the cost of his life.

"What of your mother?" he said, stalling for time.

Herod grimaced. "Believe me, I will not linger long after informing Mother of the arrangements."

Cypros would raise an unholy ruckus when she learned Avda would be attending to her daughter-in-law instead of treating her countless *ailments*. Herod normally went out of his way to please his beloved mother. That he was willing to risk her health and happiness spoke volumes. He was also dividing his household into those he trusted and those he did not.

Avda now belonged in the camp of those deemed suspect or disloyal.

"I am simply a physician," Avda said, his mouth dry as ground bone. "And nothing more."

But Herod's attention shifted to his brother. "We still must speak with the commander of my army. Come," he ordered striding out of the room.

Pheroras slunk to the door, pausing he looked back. He laughed bleakly. "We both know there is no such thing as *simple* for the brother and the physician to the king." Then he too was gone.

The silence that ensued was far from peaceful. Any escape from Herod must be handled carefully and discreetly. Timing would be vital. How soon was too soon to make his move? Aside from his sons, who else could he trust?

Kitra.

He had faith in Kitra. She was the last person in the world who would betray him. She was also the last person he should go to for help.

CHAPTER 23

Following Niv through the royal suite, Avda was too disgusted and angry with Herod to be afraid by this second summons of the night.

An ugly orange smeared the morning sky outside the window of Herod's bedchamber. An oil lamp sputtered next to a plate of untouched, congealing food. The bed covers remained undisturbed. Herod had exchanged his kingly robes for sturdy military attire.

The sight of Sohemus gave Avda pause. A longtime Herod loyalist, Sohemus' taste for ugly-colored clothing made him the target of unkind jests from his fellow servile flatterers.

Herod sank onto the edge of the bed and waved for them to be seated on a pair of wooden chairs.

Sohemus plopped his mustard-brown-swathed body onto the seat.

"Why am I here?" Avda folded his arms and stood his ground.

"Mariamne's part in this sorry affair with her grandfather has gutted me." Herod stared back with anguished eyes. "I want to trust her, but how can I after this latest deception?"

"How, indeed?" Sohemus clucked his tongue.

"Why would she betray me thus, Avda?" Herod asked in agony. "Does she care so little for me?"

Avda sealed his lips. Sohemus was welcome to tread the battleground that was Herod's volatile relationship with his wife.

Herod exploded to his feet. "I expect you both to be vigilant during my absence and watch for any further deceits or trickery on the part of my wife and mother-in-law."

"Certainly," Sohemus said hurriedly.

"And you, Avda?"

There was no denying Mariamne and Aalexis' reckless actions had played a part in last evening's tragedy. That is what came of a household, royal or not, infested with backstabbing, suspicion, and malice. And so the battle continued.

Avda stared out the window into the blinding yellow of the rising sun. Herod had been like an older brother. How had they come to this point? Were trust and fidelity gone for forever?

He met the king's harsh gaze. "As always, I will be faithful to the health and welfare of those in my care."

"Sohemus will have charge over Mariamne and Fortress Alexandrium." Herod's voice was cold as death. "You are not to interfere."

Sohemus chortled hyena-like. "I am so very ho—"

"His word will be the ultimate authority," Herod said.

It was happening again. Just as when Herod was called on the carpet before Marc Antony. He was going to leave instructions for Sohemus to execute Mariamne if matters went badly in Rhodes.

"Do not give the order," Avda pleaded.

"You are not to interfere," the king barked. "Do I make myself clear?"

Rage and disgust collided. "Perfectly."

Herod slashed the air with his hand. "Go, Avda. We are done here."

Victorious, Sohemus grinned.

Let him smirk. Avda would not trade places with the fool for all the gold in the world. Sohemus would be wise to keep his hideous mud-colored cloak handy for the day the king turned on him and his head ended up on a pole.

But what to do about Queen Mariamne?

Avda felt the same helplessness that came when called to the bed of an incurably ill child.

Should he warn the queen? Or keep silent and hope she never learned of this second betrayal? Would anyone be able to save Mariamne if Herod's fierce jealousy turned deadly?

CHAPTER 24

Plagued by an uneasiness she could not explain, one that had made for a night of restless sleep, Elizabeth sensed something was terribly wrong the moment she and James stepped into the banquet hall for the morning meal.

Stricken-faced palace guests huddled in small groups and whispered together. Slaves moved about silent as ghosts. The somber cloud associated with death smothered the chamber.

The members of the royal family were conspicuously absent.

Her insides roiled as Niv crept to James's side. "Did you hear?"

"Out with it," James demanded.

Elizabeth drew her clasped hands tighter to her body in preparation for the grave news.

"*He* executed High Priest Hyrcanus last night." Niv's bloodshot eyes competed with his freckles for attention. In a hushed voice, he relayed the ghastly details, and ended with a frown. "*He* wants to speak to you. Now."

Her knees went weak. More murder. *He* was killing again. If King Herod did not hesitate to kill High Priests, who was safe? Being a member of the Sanhedrin had not saved her father. Who would be next? James? Her brothers?

If only Gabriel were present. He could be counted on to be a steady rock in storm and turmoil.

James spoke in her ear. "I will keep you safe, Libi. You and the rest of your family."

His reassurance proved a comfort. Which was surely evidence they were both unhinged, as was Herod.

"What if Herod knows?" Eight long days had passed since James agreed to join ranks with Phaedra and Saul, and she had not been able to stop worrying and wondering if they had committed a terrible mistake.

"Shh," James warned, his eyes scanning the room. "*He* has spies everywhere." He turned back to Niv. "Any word from your friends?"

The young slave shook his head. Niv was serving as the go-between with Saul and Phaedra. "I thought it best to consult you first."

Elizabeth dearly wished different slaves had made the journey to the winter palace. Why James had no qualms about entrusting their safety to sly Niv, whose chief talent was the ability to sneak spider-like about the palace, was beyond her.

"Very good," James said. "Go find out what they know, then wait for me in the East Hallway."

Niv turned to obey, but James grabbed his arm. "Where can I find the king?"

"The stables."

"Do you know what he wants with me?"

"No." Niv's voice held an apology. "Only that you are to report without delay."

James released him and led the way to an exit.

"Our rooms are the other way," Libi protested.

He whisked her out of the room. "I am taking you with me."

A cold draft rushed through the empty hallway. She dug in her heels. "I would rather not."

"I need you." His distracted look said he was occupied with the coming interview.

Selfish man. She would rather eat her own vomit than spend a moment in Herod's loathsome presence. "No. You do not."

"I do."

"Why?"

"I do not trust anyone to keep you safe, except myself and maybe Physician Hama. But there is no time to track down Hama."

His genuine concern dampened her ire. "If *he* turns against me, or you, there will be no safety anywhere here."

"Libi, I know what I am doing."

She almost regretted that the scared boy he had been no longer existed. Almost. "If my presence is really necess—"

"Phaedra and Saul might have betrayed us. In which case, your testimony regarding their dealings with Cleopatra could change the tide in our favor."

She hated the intrigues. Hated not knowing who to trust. "What other reason could Herod have for summoning you?"

James grew as somber as a man contemplating crucifixion.

"Nothing more than guesses, but I make it a habit to be prepared for disaster."

◆ ◆ ◆

Under ordinary circumstances, Elizabeth would enjoy watching the stable boys bustling about saddling horses for a large travel party. The odor of horse, hay, and dung was not the cause of her nausea. The suspense of waiting to learn the reason for Herod's summons was unbearable. And James was not acting like himself. He was not offering his usual remarks on the quality of the building's design and craftsmanship.

She rubbed her chilled arms. "Your pacing is making the horses nervous."

He halted. "Fickle Fortuna, where is he?"

"Who me?" King Herod led a gray-speckled war horse from the dark recesses. "You are the very image of your father, scowling like an old woman the way Simeon used to."

James's features hardened. "Did you call me here to insult me?"

Herod replied with a bleak laugh. "Hardly. You and your brother-in-law are among the few who championed my continued reign."

Elizabeth's head snapped up. Brother-in-law? Was he speaking of Gabriel?

Dour-faced Andrew stepped out of the shadows.

The brief bud of hope morphed into a choking vine. Worried over Phaedra and Saul conspiring against them, she had not considered the possibility of Andrew dealing a treacherous blow. And how unfair and unkind to jump to the worst conclusion. His presence could be completely innocent.

"Andrew, I did not—"

"Silence, woman." Andrew's voice was rife with disdain.

"My wife will be treated with respect." James's icy gaze

would freeze the River Jordan.

Bless James for his swift and ardent defense. If her brother had a speck of sense, he would heed the warning. She forced herself to look at Herod.

"If the king does not object to my presence, I will remain by my husband's side."

"Please stay. It is not as if there are any secrets in the palace." Herod stroked the enormous gray horse's neck. "What do you think of my new mount? I could construct many luxury baths with the coins I used to purchase this beautiful beast."

Fright warred with her repulsion over his easy manner in the wake of murdering High Priest Hyrcanus. She rubbed her clammy palms together. "He appears quite able of carrying a rider wishing to flee trouble."

James coughed loudly and stepped in front of her. "A summons from the king tends to be unsettling."

"That is a truth I cannot argue with," Herod replied, unperturbed. "I have been called to Rhodes. I am taking a contingent of supporters prepared to testify on my behalf. Andrew has offered to accompany me to represent the Temple officers. Can I expect your support?"

Elizabeth bit the soft flesh on the inside of her lower lip. *No. Never,* her mind screamed.

"Only if my wife is welcomed also," James answered.

"Of course." Herod smiled. "She will enjoy the company of Saul and Phaedra Boethus who happily accepted my invitation."

James glanced back at her, his thumb rubbing over his fading scar. "What do you say, Wife?"

What a perfect, nasty, entangling web. James and Andrew standing as character witnesses for Herod of Idumea minus High Priest Hyrcanus's execution would have been distasteful. To do so now would taint them with the blood of a frail old man.

The supporters of Queen Mariamne and the Hasmoneans would offer John's murder as proof Herod meant to eliminate any and all potential rivals for the throne. The Herodians would point to John's secret correspondence and escape plan aided and abetted by Herod's enemies as an act of treason.

What a prize Herod would gain in claiming the support of members of aristocratic priestly lines like the Onias family represented by James and Andrew. Meanwhile, priests belonging to more humble stock who hated the corrupt practices of the elite Temple officers would be outraged beyond measure.

James's brow creased as the silence stretched.

King Herod and Andrew watched her closely.

How could she even pretend to support a man who did not fear the Lord or have respect for the Lord's people? Or pretend to support the man who had killed her father?

But to snub Herod might well prove deadly.

Clutching her hands together to still her trembling anger, she nodded her agreement.

Herod urged the war horse forward and drew James and Andrew along as he gave travel instructions.

Elizabeth remained frozen in place. Herod had not won. Not yet.

The Romans might unseat him. How she prayed they would.

If not—

A seed of a plan bloomed.

An exciting solution.

As a first step, she would send a letter to Lydia and Kadar and hope James's sister and brother-in-law would agree to help.

CHAPTER 25

J ames helped Elizabeth down from the royal carriage Herod had provided to carry them from the winter palace to Jerusalem.

There would be no time to rest, and hardly time to pack before setting out for Rhodes. The arrangement suited him—the less time he spent in the cloying city and this monstrosity of a house the better. The sight of Libi's rumpled attire pricked his conscience. "We could sail on a later ship to give you more time to prepare."

"I do not need more time," she murmured, holding tight to Apollo.

If she did not recover from her pensive silence, the two to three-week land and sea journey would be unbearable. He touched her sleeve. "Talk to me."

Apollo growled and clawed his hand.

He sucked on his bloody finger. "Stop that cat!"

Libi stroked Apollo. "Your loud voice irritates him."

The cat was welcome to go to Hades. His concern was all for Libi. "I know you are not happy with the trip to Rhodes. But all will be well."

"How?" she demanded. "Did you miss the stares of distrust, revulsion, and contempt aimed at the royal procession? Do you not see the judgmental faces of your neighbors?"

"Our neighbors," he corrected. The same peevish tone had marked his youth. "Fickle Fortuna, my father's house never fails but to bring out the worst in me."

"Or is it easier to blame a building or a place than your own failings?" Sorrow glistened in Elizabeth's eyes.

A cold breeze slapped his face. He glanced around at his childhood surroundings.

Benjamin and Banna's grandfather Jachim sat bundled up in his usual spot behind a low garden wall. His cheeks and nose were bright pink, but the old man would not retreat inside until witnessing the smoke rise from the Evening Offering. Jachim's expression was neither hostile or friendly, which could mean his mind was no longer sharp or he had concluded James was a lost cause. Phillip Peter and Martha sneered at him from the doorway of their palatial home, a house paid for with riches coming from their exclusive rights to provide unblemished animals to Temple worshipers. And Rabbi Gabini practically held his nose as he marched his students down the narrow street.

Why would he care about the judgment of his neighbors?

Jachim untangled an arm from a heavy woolen blanket and beckoned James to come near.

Tempted to ignore the summons, James looked back at Elizabeth. "Do you mind?"

"Why ask, when you always do as you please?"

Their front door banged open and the slave Saad peered out. A smile lit his wizened face. "Master James and Mistress Elizabeth, you should have sent word you were coming, and I would have made sure your bedchamber was toasty warm."

Elizabeth set Apollo on the ground. The black cat hurried inside, passing young Marcus who flew down the stairs. "Saad has been his usual boring self, but I learned to juggle." Three brown-cloth balls sat nestled in the crook of his arm. "I can show you if you like."

At least someone was glad to see him. James ruffled the boy's uncombed hair. "Maybe later. First you need to pack a bag for a trip to Rhodes. Unless you would rather remain here with Saad."

Marcus whooped with joy and raced up the stairs, almost knocking over the old man in his rush to gather his meager belongings.

"Slow down, boy," Saad said, then he glowered at James with rheumy eyes. "I am as useless as a broken chamber pot to you now, am I?"

James held onto his patience. "I was thinking of your creaky bones and sore joints, you old fool. You would be in miserable pain before Jerusalem even faded from sight."

Elizabeth hurried up the stairs and cradled Saad's frail hand.

"James has dragged you over half the world and back. Your years of faithful service have earned you an easier, more sedate life."

"Maybe I should hurry to my death bed so as not to be a bother. I can work circles around Marcus," Saad mumbled.

"Run up and down those stairs," James said.

Libi glared at him. "Stop taunting the poor man."

"I have slowed down in recent years." Saad flexed a knee and winced.

James climbed the stairs and squeezed his shoulder. "I

command you to live to be at least one hundred. What would I do without you? None of the other servants can cook a lentil stew to compare to yours." The flattery would be wholly true if the stubborn slave could be convinced to add more salt, as he'd been directed to do countless times.

Mollified, Saad shuffled inside. Elizabeth turned to follow.

"Libi, wait."

She crossed her arms. "What more is there to say?"

"You are determined to be angry with me."

"I am not angry. Your blindness frightens me."

"Blindness?"

"I am at fault for hoping you could change."

He saw red. "Which of my *many* failings do you expect me to apologize for? My abiding anger over the roadside attack that left me scarred and unfit for priestly duties, all because of my father's selfish desire to gain the office of High Priest? Giving my support to the usurper Herod, instead of the corrupt Hasmoneans who enrich themselves at the expense of the poor and lowborn? My disgust with hypocritical *holy* men like Phillip Peter who judged me even as he pays secret visits to a harlot?"

She paled but held her head high. "I heard you were once quite fond of harlots, particularly of one called Morta."

James cringed and smoothed his tan robe. He had not found time to check on Morta to see how the likable woman fared. Time was not kind to aging harlots. He would send Niv in his stead to see if she needed food or other necessities.

"I swear my drunken, whore-mongering days are behind me."

"So you say." Elizabeth stared past him.

Her aloofness gutted him. "I am not the man I used to be."

"Jachim is waiting." She walked inside without a backward glance.

He was mightily tempted to pursue her and force her to see the matter his way, but that would only prove her point.

He trudged next door and leaned against the garden wall. The last thing James needed was a lecture disguised in the form of a long-winded story from Jachim, who as a younger man had served as a priest beside his good friend High Priest John Hyrcanus. "*Shalom*, Jachim. Congratulations on your new great grandsons. And how are the proud fathers?"

As a boy, James had spent many hours with the twin brothers. Their grandfather Jachim had seemed ancient then.

The ninety-five-year-old man held a frail mottled-brown hand to a large elongated ear. "What? I thought you said *shalom*." He clucked his tongue. "Your grandfather used to greet me the same every morning. '*Shalom*, neighbor', he would always say, after the mean-hearted hypocrite spent the entire morning yelling and berating your poor father and his good wife. You never knew the grandfather you were named for. Nothing your father did ever pleased the old goat. That is the name your father and I used behind his back."

The wall's jagged stones dug into James's gut. How many times had he referred to his father as the old goat?

"Yet my father mistreated me and my sisters horribly, even after what he had suffered."

"I pointed this truth out a time or two and was told to

keep my nose out of his affairs. Your father would not be the first man to repeat his father's mistakes." He offered James a bleak smile. "It is probably for the best you do not have a son."

The condemnation arrowed deep. "I would never…"

"Elizabeth would not allow it," Jachim said, occupied with tugging his blanket higher. "She is far stronger than your mother and grandmother."

James almost fell over from shock. "You do not disapprove of the marriage?"

Jachim brightened. "Did you hear the good news? Benjamin and Banna have newborn sons." He paused to scratch his wrinkled nose. "The one-armed boy was certainly excited."

Fickle Fortuna. The old man's mind was slipping—and here James was taking his words to heart. "Marcus was happy to learn he would be traveling to Rhodes with us."

"You are taking Elizabeth?" Jachim asked, his voice quavering.

James glanced back at the house that had always been more prison than home. "I think she would prefer to remain here and wave to you across the garden wall."

"That is perfectly understandable. She must be quite devastated."

"Must she?" James replied, preoccupied with the list of chores needing his attention before departing for Rhodes.

Jachim nodded. "Nehonya, now there was a good man."

"Elizabeth loved her father. And she was the apple of his eye." James hoped his body did not outlive his mind —trapped between memories of the past and confusion over the present.

Jachim paused from the battle with his blanket, and a

glint of clarity shone in his eyes.

"John's execution could not help but stir up memories of her father's murder at the hands of Herod," he said. "But I doubt you need me to state the obvious."

James reeled as though punched. He had to be the world's most selfish jackass. Eight years had passed since Herod had purged the Temple officers of suspected enemies, starting with Elizabeth's beloved father.

Yet James had considered only his best interests when insisting Elizabeth celebrate their wedding at a banquet hosted by the man who had murdered her father. Damnation, he had been as sensitive as a rock to her feelings. And if Herod prevailed in his bid to keep his throne and named James as his master builder, it would mean working together for years to come. The fame and glory and livelihood he sought would cost Elizabeth dearly.

He might as well rub her face in a pile of dung.

Jachim pointed to the sky. "Peace with Yahweh. Do you see?"

The smoke from the Evening Sacrifice wreathed the Temple.

James could not recall a time of peace. His whole life had been a battle.

The old man tottered to his feet and shuffled away. "Blessings on your journey, James Onias."

And James loathed himself even more because he would not be making the trip to Rhodes alone. He would not and could not leave Elizabeth behind.

CHAPTER 26

Elizabeth stood at the rail of the graceful ship plying the calm waters of the Great Sea. A warm breeze caressed her cheeks. Stars stretched endlessly overhead. The soft creak of the rigging lulled.

If only she and James were on an idyllic trip bound for a land where greed, deception, and violence were unknown, instead of sailing as guests of King Herod on his mission to persuade Rome he deserved to remain sovereign ruler of Israel.

James and Andrew emerged from Herod's private cabin and headed toward her.

Andrew grimaced upon spotting her and walked away in the opposite direction. James had urged her to not take her brother's continued hostility to heart, but his open rejection grieved her.

James's face was lost in the shadows, but he was almost certainly still in the same brooding mood plaguing him since leaving Jerusalem. At first she was relieved when he had found alternate spots to sleep, attributing his remote pensive air to preoccupation with the impending trial.

She was beginning to believe there was more to it.

He paused a short distance away. His Julian-style haircut, in need of a trim, stood on end. He avoided her eyes. "We will reach the safety of Rhodes by morning."

But would they be any safer? The hours and hours he had spent conversing alone with Herod was worrisome. She feared her husband was contemplating a dangerous or unwise move. "There is something you are not telling me."

Face haggard, he closed his eyes and swallowed. "As soon as I can arrange matters I will divorce you and you will be free to pursue a life of charity and service."

She grasped the deck rail. The ship capsizing would have come as less of a shock.

"Divorce? Is this some cruel game or trick?"

He cried out like a wounded beast and captured her in a tight embrace.

"I have treated you cruelly. But not anymore. Once we are ashore you will never have to set eyes on me again if that is your wish."

She pushed against his unyielding chest. Not see James again? The thought robbed her of breath.

"That is not my wish. Now kindly release me, before you crush me to death."

"You cannot mean it. Not after I forced a wedding banquet on you hosted by a man you hate. After my blindness to the painful memories John Hyrcanus's execution must cause. And after I insisted you attend a trial where your husband might be called upon to defend the man who murdered your father. These actions, and more, have been wholly selfish and unforgivable."

The remorseful confession brought a flood of tears. She buried her face in his solid chest. "You do understand. You do care."

His mouth pressed against her ear. "Libi, I love you more than anything in this world. But I have acted as cruelly as my father, considering my wants and desires alone. I am ashamed it took senile old Jachim to point out what should have been obvious."

She curled her fingers in a tunic made of the sturdy cloth favored by the stonecutters. He did love her. Her heart knew that much. "You are not your father."

"Is it too much to ask?" Pain echoed in his voice. "Will you exchange letters, writing to me of your life among the widows and admonishing me not to forget to smile from time to time?"

He was in earnest about the divorce and helping her pursue her heart's desire to minister to widows. Was that what she still wanted most?

"I thought you could not live without me."

A shudder quaked his shoulders. "Knowing you are happy and safe will be enough."

The future was suddenly as dark and murky as the inky black waters cradling the ship. Did she love James the way he loved her? Should she stay or escape before he changed his mind?

"I need time to consider your offer."

"Offer?" He backed away and laughed bleakly. "Fickle Fortuna, Libi. You make it sound as if we are discussing purchasing cows or sheep instead of our marriage."

"This is all very confusing." She clasped her hands to keep from reaching for him. "And comparing your wife to a cow is not the way to win her over. "

James frowned. "Are you my wife?"

She refused to meet his eyes. "We are married. So—"

He trapped her against the ship rail, captured her face, and kissed her soundly.

She gasped for breath. "Did you have to do that?"

The diagonal scar on his cheek had never made him look more severe. "If you stay, we will have a real marriage. We will be true husband and wife. Do I make myself clear?"

The truth took her by surprise. In her heart he did not hold the place of stepson or friend in time of trouble. No. She loved him. Loved him as a woman loved a man.

She wrapped her arms around his neck and pulled his mouth to hers and kissed him as a wife kissed her husband.

He returned her impassioned kisses, then groaned and set her at arm's length. "Am I misunderstanding matters? Or are you agreeing to my terms?"

She could not help but smile. "I see you have not consulted the Songs of Solomon when it comes to wooing your beloved."

"A moment ago you asked for more time," he said crankily.

This was the James she knew and loved. "Make me your true wife, Husband."

Love, hope, fear, and desire warred in his eyes. "Are you sure?"

She glanced at their cabin door, then back at the man who from all outward appearances was Roman and not Jewish. She took a deep breath. "I am sure I love you. And that will not change."

His heated mouth feathered her ear. "My sweet, sweet, Libi, I have dreamed of this night forever."

Warmth blossomed deep inside. "So have I, my love. So have I."

Her cheek resting on her husband's bare chest, Elizabeth awakened to the sounds of the sailors readying the ship to dock in the harbor of Rhodes. Barked commands and the thumps of sails being lowered drifted through the small porthole that provided cooling air to the snug berth.

"How are you?" James asked, tenderly stroking her arm.

Pleasure rippled through her. "I don't suppose we could bribe the captain to continue sailing and sailing and sailing?"

James kissed her forehead. "I was afraid I would wake to find last night was too good to be true." A long moment passed. "Are you having regrets?"

She pressed closer to him. "Absolutely not." A bride twice before, she knew regret well. The first at age thirteen to a man four times her age. And second to Saul, known as the Egyptian. "Last night was the most wonderful of my life."

He rolled her onto her back and gazed at her with apprehension. "I appreciate the compliment, but that is not what I was asking."

"You realize you saved me from disgrace—only I could manage to be married three times and still remain a virgin."

"Elizabeth," he growled.

Was it wrong to want to resist the end of this moment of happiness? Tempted to call him grumpy puppy, she drew his hand to her flat stomach.

"It is probably too much to hope we conceived a child. How—"

"Why is it too much to hope for?" A beautiful fierceness shined in onyx black eyes.

"My advanced age, for one."

"Thirty-one is not old."

Most of her friends and cousins had conceived their first children by the age of fifteen and sixteen. Their children were now having children. "Women with my condition often are childless."

His palm tenderly cupped her belly. "The Ethiopian midwife who provided your cure assured me it would heal you and make you whole."

"That would be lovely, but—"

"You will be a mother. I have always believed that." He grew distant and he rubbed his thumb over the scar on his clean-shaved cheek.

"You are thinking of your father."

"Learning he was a withered-up she goat was a happy day." Despair filled his voice. "I took great joy in taunting him. Telling him he could marry twenty more virgins and none of them would give him sons. And that I was the only son he would ever have...James the Apostate. That is the day I shaved my hair and beard."

Her heart ached for him. "You renounced your birthright as a priest of Israel to spite your father."

He shuddered. "What if we have a son as wicked as my father and grandfather—and me?"

She wrapped her arms around his neck and looked into his tortured eyes. "You are not your father. Over and over you have done good and acted with love toward me and your sisters and Saad and Marcus. You are not him."

"You are blind with love. That is your problem."

"And you are a born skeptic." She kissed his nose.

"Let us hope our children take after their mother."

The concession was a start. Hate for his father had driven him from his faith. Might love of a wife and children draw him back?

"Would you consider re-growing your beard?"

He wrinkled his nose. "That rat pelt?"

"I miss it."

"That proves you have no sense of aesthetics."

The calls of the sailors grew louder and the ship bumped to a stop. Someone banged on their cabin door and Herod's laugh penetrated the room. "Do you two intend to spend all day abed?"

"How does Herod know we are still in bed?" she whispered.

"Thin walls?"

She cringed.

Herod rapped on the door again. "By the way, if you want to win the position of master builder you should follow your wife's advice and grow your beard back. The Levite guards will never allow an apostate Jew to oversee the construction of the Temple."

"He will ask me to kiss his feet next if I am not careful," James muttered, sitting up and swinging his bare legs over the side of the berth. "Go away!"

But Herod's heavy footsteps had already moved on.

Elizabeth busied herself dressing. Everything had changed between her and James, but trouble was far from over. Simeon could no longer provoke James, but Herod's ruthless ambition loomed large, ready to incite her husband's worst instincts.

She would fight until her last breath to ensure James did not become as lost and ruthless as Herod.

CHAPTER 27

Under *protective* guard at Fortress Alexandrium for three weeks now, Avda could not complain about the accommodations—the newly rebuilt mountaintop outpost was fit for royalty—but it was impossible to feel comfortable in the knowledge the stronghold was the favored depository for those who had lost favor with King Herod.

Ori and Benjamin at least viewed the change as an adventure. They were thriving under the guidance of a new youthful, sharp-minded tutor and could not be happier with their regular hikes exploring the surrounding hills.

The daily routine Avda had established for himself kept his mind busy and helped the days pass with tolerable quickness. He spent mornings attending to the health of the royal family and dedicated afternoons to welfare of the servants and soldiers serving at the fortress. Evenings were his respite, reserved for dining with his sons and sharing stories and reading.

But the arrival of the deepest hours of the night inevitably ruined whatever strides he had made toward peace. He was plagued by visions of John Hyrcanus twisting at the end of a cloth-covered rope. And nightmares of fleeing Israel with his sons one step ahead of a vengeful Herod.

But that was preferable to the nights he woke in a fever, consumed with desire for Kitra. Longing to hold her curvaceous body, haunted by the allure of her full red lips and glossy mane of black hair, while the ghost of her exotic perfume flirted with his nose.

He gripped the strap of the leather medicine pouch slung across his chest and hurried down a deserted hallway.

This fixation with a woman he could not have must stop.

She was as safe as could be, and very likely thriving, tucked away at the magnificent desert fortress of Masada. The constant demands from Cypros and Salome would be enough to try a saint, but Kitra maneuvered the ins and outs of palace life with ease. More troublesome was the fact her father and brother were at the fortress acting as protectors and overseers of the large extended Herodian family. No doubt, they were using the time to draw up a list of potential husbands for her.

"Worry about your own troubles, Avda," he mumbled under his breath, and stalked into Queen Mariamne's elegantly appointed reception chamber.

Baby Aristobulus toddled toward him. A gummy smile and bright eyes had replaced the fevered dullness that had inflicted the poor little fellow for the past few days.

Avda smiled. "Good morning, little one."

Chubby arms hugged his legs.

He chuckled and patted the boy's back. "I am your good friend today, am I? Try to remember that the next time I need to examine your mouth and throat."

Aristobulus babbled a merry reply, then raced away to

the play area in a nearby corner furnished with child-size couches, chairs, and tables. He joined his older brother and sisters and numerous cousins, playing with bright colored wooden toys.

A cursory check of the young faces revealed no signs of runny noses or bright red cheeks.

"Physician Hama, I must speak with you," the queen said in distress, breaking away from her perpetually unhappy mother and the toady Sohemus.

Avda strode to the prison of plush couches where the trio whiled away the days. "It is not uncommon for children to be feverish when new teeth come in."

"Did you know my *loving* husband ordered Sohemus to kill me and my mother if Octavian executes him?" Animosity pinched her refined face. "Why did you not warn me? I expected better of you."

Avda would have preferred to be pelted with rocks. "The king did not confide in me."

"The cruel, cruel man," the queen wailed, frightening the children. "Insisting I go to the grave if he does. How can a wife trust such a brute?"

Her five-year-old son hurried to his mother's side in protective fashion.

Consumed with anger, the queen paced, oblivious to the boy.

What reply could Avda make? As each year passed, Herod's passionate love for Mariamne tilted more and more toward insane jealousy.

Aalexis offered Sohemus an ingratiating smile. "Thankfully we have some true friends."

Clad in a particularly hideous mucus-green tunic, Sohemus beamed at the praise.

Avda could not believe a longtime friend of Herod

could be so foolish and shortsighted.

"Do you have no regard for the king's displeasure when he learns you broke his confidence?"

What bribes had the queen and Aalexis offered to tempt Sohemus to risk his neck? Promises of spectacular wealth? An advantageous marriage. Assurances of gaining the highest reaches of power and prestige?

Sohemus shrugged. "Our good queen and her mother had guessed at the truth. It seems you are assuming Herod will not end up in an early grave."

"Amen," Aalexis added with zeal, oblivious to the fact her grandson was listening.

The fright on the boy's face broke Avda's heart.

Mariamne held out her arms to the boy. "All will be well, my darling." But her troubled expression contradicted her words. For good reason.

The beautiful chamber housed in a fortress prison was akin to lovely Mariamne trapped in marriage to her savage-minded husband. The angels help them all if she lost the power to temper Herod's worst tendencies.

The familiar sound of tinkling of bracelets echoed through the chamber.

"Why are they here?" Sohemus asked, scowling at the far side of the room.

Avda's heart beat faster.

CHAPTER 28

Kitra clasped Jazmine's small hand and hurried to keep up with her brother as he strode boldly through the fortress reception chamber, his sight set on Queen Mariamne.

The queen, her mother, Sohemus, and the children stopped and stared, but Kitra had eyes only for Avda.

Good gods.

Broad-chested and chiseled-jaw, he was the picture of manly ruggedness. How had she been blind to this attraction for so long? And how was she to return to viewing him simply as kind-hearted Physician Hama?

The heat in his eyes did not help. Her insides warmed recalling the passionate kisses they had shared at their parting. Were his dreams also filled with reliving the taste and touch of their lips?

"Physician Hama!" Jazmine broke free and ran to Avda's side. She lifted her beaming face.

A visible tremble went through Avda before he turned his attention to Jazmine. "Good day, little one. It is a surprise to see you. Why did you leave Fortress Masada and your Aunt Cypros?" He glanced up at Kitra with concerned eyes.

Jazmine scrunched her nose. "Aunt Cypros complains all day long. And Cousin Salome is cross with everyone. I was so, so, so happy when Mama told me we were going to visit my grandmother, even though we have to go a long, long, long way into the wilderness to see her."

"Remember our talk about not tattling," Kitra chided, even though in full sympathy.

She could not agree fast enough when Taj had suggested visiting their mother, but she should have known he had ulterior motives. But she had not worked to change his mind when informed Fortress Alexandrium had been added to the itinerary, had she? No, the temptation to see Avda had outweighed the concern over her brother's reckless intentions.

Jazmine poked out her lower lip. "I did not lie. Aunt Cypros is grouchy."

"Lies and tattling are not the same." Kitra fought not to smile.

Avda chuckled and patted Jazmine's head. "I see the daughter is as honest as her mother."

"Take my advice, Physician Hama," Aalexis interjected, picking at the fan resting on her lap. "Never trust the Herodians. They are all liars."

Taj winked and flashed the gorgeous grin that had seduced countless women. "Ah...but we are good at keeping secrets."

"Such as the secret you and Chaya kept from Physician Hama?" Aalexis struck, deadly as a viper.

"Mother!" Queen Mariamne cried, appalled.

Kitra gasped and her stomach pitched. Oh, that a powerful quake would split the ground and swallow them whole. It would be less devastating than Avda learning the truth about Chaya and Taj.

Avda's face drained of color. "Secrets? But Chaya was quiet and never spoke to anyone." He looked in shock at Taj. "Did you sport with my wife?"

Taj shifted and coughed a laugh. "I have a wife. Just because I cannot stand the smell of Sabina and her ten dogs does not make me an adulterer."

"Perhaps I am mistaken," Aalexis said, her voice now overly sweet.

Avda gazed at Kitra in desolation. "I do not know what to believe."

His trust sliced sharp as diamonds. She could not and would not lie to him. But the truth would be Taj's death sentence. Indecision clawed at her throat. "Jazmine needs to eat and nap."

Her daughter clasped Avda's hand. "Where are Ori and Benjamin? Mama says I should not ask to visit. I promise to eat all my food and fall fast asleep afterward."

Avda's brow furrowed. "It is for your mother to decide."

"Please," her daughter pleaded.

Brashness recovered, Taj prowled around the couches. "If there are no objections, I will make myself comfortable here." He wedged his way between Aalexis and Sohemus. "And how do you dispel the boredom at Fortress Alexandrium?"

Sohemus hopped to feet shod in puce-colored sandals. Using the excuse of needing to check on the guards, he hurried away.

Jazmine drew Avda to Kitra's side. "Tell mama you are happy to have us visit."

"Ori and Benjamin will be sorely disappointed if you do not come see them."

Avda smelled of spices and herbs and all that was good

and clean. Whereas Taj reeked of seduction, greed, and ambition. The past could not be undone, but she would do the right thing by Avda now. He would hear the truth about Taj and Chaya from her.

"I will not deny the boys a visit. I know how fond they are of Jazmine."

"And you." Kindness warmed his voice. "In their nightly prayers, the boys ask the Lord to watch over you as well as Jazmine."

"How sweet. You and the boys were never far from our thoughts."

Affection shone in his eyes. "I cannot tell you how much that pleases me."

Guilt pulsed through her. She took Jazmine's hand. "Shall we go see Ori and Benjamin?"

Ensconced between them, Jazmine chirped happily as Avda led the way.

She glanced back at Taj. Leaving him to his own devices was not wise. But the private conversation with Avda was likely to be brief. And excruciatingly painful.

CHAPTER 29

After departing the queen's reception chamber with Kitra and Jazmine, Avda found his sons on the bleak slope beneath the fortress's western wall on a rock-collecting expedition with their enthusiastic young tutor.

Jazmine happily joined in the *treasure* hunt, and the bobbing heads of the foursome disappeared over an adjacent hill.

Avda and Kitra struck out in the opposite direction.

A hawk circled the leaden sky.

The jangle of Kitra's bangles shattered the silence as they picked their way across the barren landscape.

He halted on a rocky precipice. Dread ate at his gut.

"Is it true? Chaya engaged in affair with Taj behind my back?"

The wind whipped Kitra's black mane across her sorrowful face. "Taj was all to blame."

Grief and guilt tore at his heart. The marriage to Chaya was not the love match he had enjoyed with the boys' mother, but he believed her to share his contentment.

"How could I not know Chaya was unhappy with me and our marriage? I tried to be attentive and loving, but obviously I failed."

"The fault is not yours." Kitra hugged her middle.

"Infernal flames! I was her husband and yet I did not suspect a single thing was wrong."

Kitra's pitying look sliced sharp as a scalpel.

"Seducing married women is my brother's favorite sport. The purer and more innocent the victim and the more good and noble the husband the greater his triumph."

"Was I the only one blind to the affair? Or did the whole palace know?"

"If Taj was not discreet, he would have been killed long ago," she assured him.

"Aalexis seemed quite smug in her knowledge." He kicked a stone down the steep incline.

"Rumors occasionally swirl with this and that woman named. Aalexis' accusation was most likely a chance guess. You know the amount of satisfaction she and Queen Mariamne get from needling us Herodians."

"I do," he growled, sick to death of the endless hateful sniping between the two families. "How could Chaya betray me and the boys for Taj?"

"I am so sorry." She drew closer.

The sympathy was misplaced. Palace life had not suited tender-hearted Chaya, yet his loyalty to Herod had outweighed his consideration for his wife's happiness. And how many nights had he spent at the bedside of the sick rather than with Chaya?

"Did Chaya and Taj love each other?" He shuddered like one of his patients when he suggested the use of a maggot cure. He owed it to Chaya to try to understand the whole ugly truth.

Kitra returned his pained look. "I cannot speak for

Chaya's heart, but I can say love did not figure in it for my brother. If it is any consolation, Taj's flirtations never last long. After the conquests he quickly grows bored."

"You knew, but never said a word to me?"

Her lovely face paled. "Taj insists on bragging to me, after the fact, even though I have begged him time and again not to confide his shameful exploits. I wish I could say I kept the secret only to save you and your sons the pain, but I also had selfish reasons. I feared you would hate and despise me. And seek revenge against Taj."

Avda stared up at the towering fortress where Taj was attempting to worm his way into Queen Mariamne's good graces, just as he had beguiled Chaya with flattering words and flirtatious winks. His sick game had ended with Chaya taking her own life. Did it matter if it was out of grief for lost love or shame over her sin?

Avda's hands tightened into fists. "I should kill him."

Kitra clasped his arm. "Taj does not deserve mercy, but I beg it of you nonetheless. He is my only ally and I love him."

Could he take a life? The other choice would be to accuse Taj of adultery before a judge. It would require finding witnesses, but any credible witnesses would have stepped forward at the time. Confiding in Herod was not an option, as the king's insane jealousy could put Mariamne in as much jeopardy as Taj.

"I will do nothing for now." He exhaled heavily. He would give the problem more thought. Perhaps consult with someone shrewder. James Onias's name came to mind.

Tears stained Kitra's eyes. "I hope you can find it in your heart to forgive me for clinging to my love for my brother."

Who was he to judge? How many times had he defended and sided with Herod when his friend was clearly in the wrong or committed an evil?

"There is nothing to forgive." He kissed her forehead.

She trembled and smiled weakly. "You are a good, good man, Avda."

He might be a good man, but he had been a poor husband to Chaya. And all his healing knowledge had not saved his beloved Mary from bleeding to death after delivering Benjamin.

What made him think he could protect Kitra from the constant deadly palace intrigues after failing so miserably before? And how foolish to believe a woman who had been married to a prince would be content to start a new life in a distant land as the wife of a simple physician.

Besides, he must see to his sons' best interests. If by some miracle Kitra's greedy, ambitious father allowed the marriage, it would throw the boys into the realm of a family he could not respect, not to mention make Taj his brother-in-law.

He stepped back. A blast of freezing wind raked his neck. "Go collect Jazmine, then inform your brother he must leave immediately and depart from Israel permanently after the visit with your mother."

Misery erased all signs of Kitra's normal vivaciousness. "We will never meet again, will we?"

"It is for the best," he said, although losing her would rip a gaping hole in his heart.

She dipped her head. "Is it too much to ask, will you remember me kindly?"

"Always," he said voice rough with emotion.

He would never forget Kitra.

170

CHAPTER 30

T he sky over Rhodes was its usual bright blue, but a shifting wind played havoc on the seabirds wheeling overhead and the small fishing boats plying the choppy waters below. The stone causeway encircling the harbor teamed with busy merchants, boisterous sailors, sweat-drenched dock workers, wandering beggars, and market shoppers.

Closer at hand, dirt-smudged schoolboys shouted with glee and spread out over the ruins of the famed Colossus of Rhodes. Herod was among those scaling a giant bronze-plated, iron-reinforced hand. The king took his turn trying to wrap his arms around a massive thumb. He grinned at James. "Each finger is the size of a regular statue."

The harbor continued to fascinate despite the numerous inspections they had made of the site since their arrival on the Greek isle one week ago. The statue once towered over the harbor. What a sight that must have been, but it had been toppled by an earthquake some two hundred years ago. Rome had sacked Rhodes a few years earlier, carrying off thousands of statues. But evidence of the island's former grandeur abounded.

James gave a thumbs-up signal, marveling at Herod's relaxation in spite of the coming trial that would decide all their fates.

The king abandoned the statue and scrambled up the embankment, rejoining James. "Are you going to spend the entire day fretting over your wife?"

Elizabeth had begged off making the trek, preferring to spend a quiet morning in the palatial gardens of the once magnificent home hosting Herod's travel party. Not that she would enjoy much peace with chatty young Marcus as a companion.

James worked his mouth. How could he feel at ease wondering what mischief Saul and Phaedra might be up to on their unexpected side trip to Egypt? On the bright side, his chief rival for master builder was missing out on the opportunity to capture Herod's ear as he indulged in his passion for construction and building design. "Whereas, you have not spared a moment's thought for *your* wife."

Herod grunted. "Women problems will be the death of me."

"I have only one woman to please. I do not know how you manage a house full."

"By housing them in separate fortresses as a start." Herod laughed his chagrin. "If I want any peace, I might have to make the arrangement permanent."

Ominous dark clouds boiled up on the horizon. James pointed at a white-sailed merchant ship racing for the safety of the port.

"Can you imagine how rough the sea would be without the addition of the breakwater?" he said.

"Precisely," Herod said enthusiastically. "If Israel is to truly prosper, we need a proper harbor. We could construct something similar. Caesarea has real possibilities. I have visions for an aqueduct, palace, and theater, and much more."

James salivated over the prospect of constructing glittering cities out of the dust. The task would require a lifetime of work, year after year of collaboration with King Herod.

The question that had been torturing him ever since the disturbing chat with his elderly neighbor stabbed his conscience. Could he do that to Libi? Her composure these past weeks gave him no comfort. Just as her steady strength put him to shame.

The sky darkened, and the wind tore at his tunic. The determined merchant boat clawed against the rise and fall of the surging swells. Shipwrecks were as common as pestilence and disease, but the prospect of watching men drown proved disturbing.

"I suggest we seek cover."

"A tumultuous storm does the heart good," Herod shouted above the roar of the wind as he lifted a gleeful face and opened his arms.

How did you tell a king he was foolish? "Get drenched if you will, but I—"

"Master James!" a young voice called out. One-armed Marcus hustled past the last of the dilapidated warehouses and ran along the sea wall.

Sandals slapping on stone, James rushed to intercept the boy. "What's wrong? Where is Mistress Elizabeth?"

They met at the base of a steep stairway leading to a temple dedicated to Helios. Marcus gasped for breath.

"Mistress Elizabeth went out for a walk."

"Alone?" James asked, imagining her the victim of all manner of evil. *Stubborn, vexing woman.* He should not have trusted her safety to anyone but himself. "I ordered you not to let my wife out of your sight."

Tears pooled in Marcus's eyes. "She insisted. I secretly followed her for a short while, but decided it was best to find you. She is with those strange-dressed people. Paul and...I mean Saul. And Ph.... You know, that odd woman and her brother."

Hell and crucifixion, what did Phaedra and Saul want with Elizabeth?

"You did well. You did right." James blindly patted the boy on the back.

Herod joined them. His eyes were as black and stormy as the sea. "Is there trouble?"

James fought to control his raging emotions. His panic might be unfounded. Phaedra and Saul asking Libi out for a walk could be totally innocent. For all he knew they might be passing on well-wishes to Elizabeth from shared Egyptian acquaintances. Or entrusting information pertaining to Aalexis. Or seeking an update on how matters stood with Herod.

He smoothed his wind-ruffled robe. "Elizabeth was concerned I would not have good sense enough to get out of the storm."

Herod laughed uproariously. "She knows you well. Go calm your wife. I am going to find the driest spot available to watch the deluge."

James forced his mouth to form a smile. "Come, Marcus. It is never wise to worry your wife unnecessarily." He led the boy away. It took all his might to walk at a steady pace.

King Herod remained on the seawall, legs braced against the battering wind. He clapped and cheered as the merchant ship slid through the harbor opening into the calmer port waters.

Reaching the shadows of an ancient grain warehouse, James took off at a run down a long dark alley. Fat raindrops pelted his face.

For the first time in years, he prayed to the Lord God of Israel. *Please let Elizabeth be safe.*

CHAPTER 31

The bustling market emptied of buyers as merchants took refuge in their booths to wait out the fast approaching storm. Elizabeth kept expecting Saul and Phaedra to flee to avoid the ruin of the black kohl lining their eyes and the dabs of ocher coloring their cheeks. But brother and sister strolled at a leisurely pace past bins of wilting herbs, over-ripe melons, and dirty red beets.

"Did you have the opportunity to visit with any of your friends?" she asked, hoping to learn why the couple had made the brief visit to Egypt. And she wondered anew why the pair had asked her out for a walk.

Phaedra brushed past a frayed basket holding a clutch of shriveled oranges and struck out toward a deserted plaza. The wind tugged at her pleated tunic. Her smile was as fake as the dye coloring her hair. "I'm curious. When did you learn we were plotting with Cleopatra to poison Herod?"

A cold sweat beaded Elizabeth's brow. She hurried to catch up to her former sister-in-law. "I do not understand."

Reaching a fountain featuring a naked statue of a heathen god, Phaedra whirled around and stabbed a finger at her. "Playing innocent will not save you."

Raindrops splattered the paving stones.

Saul's habit of stroking his goatee gave away his nervousness. "I told Phaedra you would not betray us. But we could not take the risk."

"So you made it look as if I was in an adulterous affair with Jonah?"

"Jonah knew too much." Phaedra made a sour face. "It is a pity. The dear boy was my most entertaining husband until he got too nosy for his own good."

The plummeting temperature was not wholly responsible for the chill raising the flesh on Elizabeth's arms.

"What threat did you use against Jonah to convince him to cooperate?"

A rosy color rose on Saul's cheeks beneath his heavy makeup. "We learned Jonah had—"

"Enough about Jonah," Phaedra commanded, then directed a sweet smile at Elizabeth. "Saul was always fond of you. And I have great admiration for your fortitude and bravery. Parting with you will break my heart."

A band of unsavory-looking men rushed the fountain from all sides.

"Ah... here they are and right on time," Phaedra cooed. "James will be crushed when he learns his precious Libi was killed by bandits."

Fear clawed at Elizabeth's throat. "Why...why are you doing this?"

Phaedra clucked her tongue. "We cannot have you running to Herod and tattling on us, now can we? That would ruin our plans for James."

"What plans?"

"It seems James knows a harlot, who knows a soldier,

who knows a camel herder who knows how to come by a tasteless, odorless poison."

Saul smiled. "A fact a judge might find very interesting when Herod dies of poisoning."

Who else knew of James's plan to poison his father? "Did Niv betray James or the harlot Morta?"

Phaedra barked a husky laugh. "The dear boy was most helpful. Especially as I made it clear marrying a red-headed husband held great appeal."

Elizabeth wrinkled her nose in disgust. "Niv might not be so pleased if he knew how you have disposed of your five previous husbands?"

"That is just another reason you need to die," Phaedra said and waved the bandits forward. She addressed the leader of the ruffians. "Remember to make it look as though you attacked us too."

Wearing a torn tunic much too large, the bandit flashed a black-toothed smile. "You are an odd pair."

Saul looked down his long nose as though inspecting a rat. "The captain of the merchant ship awaiting your arrival has been instructed not to give you the second half of your reward until you reach Carthage."

"I beg you not to do this." Elizabeth grabbed Saul's manicured hand.

"I want to go home to Ruth and construct the lovely ornamental garden we talked and dreamed of." He pulled his hand free and retreated. "They promised to make your death quick and painless. I wish I could do more."

The bandits closed in. Dressed in rags and covered in sores, they possessed the desperate edge of men with nothing to lose.

Phaedra and Saul sent up an impressive caterwauling wail.

Elizabeth backed against the slippery stone edge of the fountain basin. She would fight to her last breath to escape and warn James.

Above the splashing of the fountain she heard a voice calling her name.

Cursing her short stature, she stood on tiptoes straining to see over the heads of the bandits. "Husband!"

Her mouth dropped open. James was nowhere to be found.

No, it was the giant blond barbarian Kadar who rumbled toward her, knocking bandits aside as if swatting away flies.

He reached her in a few long strides, turned his massive back to her, and planted his feet. "Who wants to take me on first?"

The men fled in all directions. Their guttural cries of fright broke through Elizabeth's initial shock.

Kadar's booming laugh echoed through the plaza. "Go ahead and run, you cowards."

The skies opened and the rain poured down.

Kadar unclasped his cape and draped it over her shoulders. "Let's get you to shelter."

"You came?" Elizabeth said, still bewildered. "I did not expect you to be here, much less rescue me."

Lydia joined them, all smiles despite the soaking rain. "Nothing could have kept us away. We left Napoli as soon as we received your letter."

Tears of joy mixed with the raindrops. Elizabeth welcomed Lydia's embrace.

Kadar pointed across the plaza, where Phaedra and Saul were scurrying down an alley. "Should I stop them?"

"No." She would rather not set eyes on them ever again.

James would no doubt feel quite differently.

"James will be overjoyed to see you." She smiled brightly at Kadar and Lydia.

CHAPTER 32

Soaked to the bone after running through half of Rhodes in search of Elizabeth, James burst into the suite assigned to them. Herod's entourage was staying in what had at one time been among the most opulent homes in Rhodes before the Roman sack of the city.

Although informed of the bandit attack by the guardsmen who had tracked him down, he did not dare to believe the report Libi was safe and sound until he saw her with his own eyes.

Wrapped in a fleece shawl, she was seated on a couch in front of the wall-size fireplace. Her smile was the most beautiful sight he had ever seen.

"James, look who I ran into?"

"You could have been killed or—"

"I will explain after you greet our guests."

Lydia and Kadar rose from the threadbare couch opposite Libi's.

"It was you? You rescued Libi?"

In hindsight the guardsman's excited description of the giant blond warrior who had stopped the attack perfectly described Kadar. James continued to stare at them and then at the four youngsters playing with toys in a corner of the room. Lydia and Kadar's children. His nephews and nieces.

And the youth standing in Kadar's shadow would be James's namesake "Little James", who now went by the name Judas.

The scar on his cheek hummed. The youth's father had been the leader of the band of zealots who had abducted Lydia and forced her to cut James's face.

Lydia beamed with pride as she looked up at her son. "Judas wants to be a master builder, don't you darling?"

The image of Judas the Zealot, the young man blushed and shifted in place. A closer inspection revealed he had his mother's large brown eyes but not his father's fiery crazed orbs. "Not now, Mother," he whispered.

Lydia hugged her son, beaming with pride. "My fondest wish is to see Judas study with the world's finest master builder. Please say you will consider it."

James was humbled. "I would count it an honor." He squeezed Judas's thin shoulder. "I do not have to tell you your father's side of the family will strongly disapprove of you working closely with their sworn enemy, King Herod."

"I am sorry it will displease my uncles." Judas's soft answer indicated a kind spirit. "But I must live my life and they must live theirs."

If Judas had a talent for building design and construction, that would be a side benefit. James did not work well with other, but he had high hopes the boy would be a much-needed assistant. "Do you have any drawings you would care to share?"

"A few, Uncle." Judas's face turned brighter red. "Actually, more than a few."

James already found much to like in him. "Spoken like a true master builder."

Lydia's smile lit the room and she opened her arms. "I am waiting for my hug, dear brother."

If anyone should be blushing it was James. Blushing in shame. Though he had resided in Rome and she in Napoli, Italy these past ten years, he had gone out of his way to avoid meeting. It was not because he had been haunted by memories of Judas the Zealot. No. But because it pained him to be reminded of his cowardice and his hateful treatment of his sisters and Elizabeth during those darkest of days. Proving he was a coward indeed.

Her forgiveness and love were a gift he could never repay. "*Shalom*, Sister. I am sorry I never responded to your letters. It was utter selfishness on my part. I would hug you if I was not wet as a homeless dog."

She laughed and kissed him on both cheeks. "Blessings on your marriage. I am so happy for you and Elizabeth."

He glanced at Libi, who was smiling beatifically. He kissed Lydia's cheek. "Your approval means the world to us."

"How could I disapprove?" She gazed lovingly at Kadar. "I understand what it is to follow your heart."

Kadar nudged him. "Do you have any affection to spare for your barbarian brother-in-law?"

James embraced the man responsible for saving his sisters, Libi, and him from Judas the Zealot and for rescuing Libi today from bandits. "I hate to think what might have been if you had not come along."

"We barely made it to the harbor ahead of the storm." Kadar owned a fleet of merchant ships. "One of my retired captains owns several market booths. I planned to ask the man if he knew of King Herod's whereabout."

"You are making a habit of coming to our aid." James cringed at the thought of Lydia and Kadar caught at the mercy of the raging storm. "I do not have enough words to express my relief and thanks."

Kadar thumped his back. "You might not be so pleased when you learn we plan to travel on to Jerusalem with you."

James clapped Kadar's muscled arm and stepped back. "Kadar the Righteous Proselyte and James the Apostate, proof God—or I should say *the gods*—make merry at our expense." The uproar in Jerusalem would be spectacular. "The gossips and chief hypocrites will have more reason to squawk over the beastly and debased Onias family."

"James..." Libi scolded.

Kadar shrugged. "I promised my wife we would make a pilgrimage with our children to worship the Lord at his holy Temple. If my presence will cause an uproar, I will —"

"We will worship as a family," Lydia said, her chin lifted high.

His sister's confidence was a testimony to her victory over their cruel father. It was also a witness to Kadar's love. James envied them and was ashamed at his own behavior.

"Sister, would you do me the great favor of accompanying Elizabeth to the Woman's Court." He met Kadar's blue eyes. "Would you be so good as to offer sacrifices on Libi's behalf?"

Libi frowned. "It is too much to ask."

"Nothing would make us happier." Lydia clasped her hand.

"It would be an honor," Kadar said.

A wail came from the children's corner. Lydia's youngest daughter had tripped and banged both knees on the stone floor. Rotten uncle that he was, James did not know or remember the names of his assorted nieces and nephews.

"Elizabeth, tell James what you told us about the bandit attack," his sister said, then left to attend to the child.

More frightened than angry, James examined his wife closely for signs of harm. "What possessed you to go with Phaedra and Saul?"

She chewed on her lip for a long moment. "You will fall ill if you do not change out of those wet clothes."

He had sent young Marcus to change into dry clothes. If the mischievous imp had not been waylaid by an adventure, he should have a fresh tunic laid out for James. He plucked at his damp tunic. "I am waiting for an answer."

She glanced uneasily at Kadar and the boy Judas. "We should speak in private."

Kadar signaled for Judas to follow him.

"No, stay," James said. "I will not have you walking blindly into danger. And Judas should know what he is getting into as my apprentice. I will not blame you if you turn for home posthaste after you hear the wasp's nest of intrigues embroiling us."

Kadar folded his arms, exposing the war wound that had put an end to his soldiering days. But with the leather tie binding his shoulder-length blond hair, he still looked every bit the formidable warrior.

"We are family. And families stick together through good and bad. We eat meals together. Worship together. Celebrate together. And we fight for one another."

"Family stands together," Judas concurred.

Kadar smiled approvingly, then his gaze sharpened.

"What are we up against?"

James felt shame for the times he had mocked the barbarian Kadar—a man much nobler than him or his father. "Libi and I cannot tell you how grateful we are to have your help."

The child soothed, Lydia rejoined them. "Is life at the palace as dangerous as rumor says?"

Libi sighed. "Israel is not at war, but that does not mean Jerusalem is at peace."

"I was guilty of charging into the center of the mess," James confessed.

A short while later, Kadar, Lydia, and Judas wore appropriately sober grimaces after learning of their tangled alliance with Phaedra and Saul and Aalexis.

"Tell James." Lydia reached for Libi's hand.

His jaw clenched. "Tell me what?"

Libi looked thoroughly miserable as she shared the details of the second attempt on her life and news of Niv's betrayal.

"The damnable pair was using us all along." Fury heated James's chest. "That will teach me to show mercy."

Libi's face turned white as alabaster. "No real harm was done. And now we know the truth."

"I will wring Niv's lying throat when I catch up to him."

"Phaedra took advantage of Niv." Libi appealed to Lydia and Kadar for support. "Revenge is not the answer. Tell him."

"You would be copying your enemy's sin," Lydia said.

"Vengeance is mine says the Lord," Kadar said, but his eyes were not unsympathetic.

James strode to the door. A lecture from the scriptures

was the last thing he wanted to hear. Libi would not be safe until Phaedra and Saul met their demise. A truth his tender-hearted wife and sister did not want to admit. He had no such qualms. The only question—how to carry out the task of sending the unscrupulous couple quickly to their graves.

"Where are you going?" Fear clouded Libi's eyes.

"To track down the Egyptian and his sister." He followed his wet tracks back outside and welcomed the lashing wind hitting his face.

Kadar joined him. "What will you do if you find them?"

"You do not want to know."

"Turn them over to Herod."

"Would you if it was Lydia?"

Kadar grew grim-mouthed. "Where do you want to start the search?"

James stared into the gathering darkness. They were not the only ones facing a long night. He doubted Herod would sleep a wink as he contemplated tomorrow's trial.

CHAPTER 33

Unsuccessful in tracking down Phaedra and Saul the evening before, James drummed a finger on his leg and watched the entrances to the uninspired reception chamber-turned-courtroom from his seat on the benches lining the walls. Like the rest of Rhodes, the governor's palace had seen better days.

Would the bloodthirsty couple dare show up at Herod's trial? Libi was convinced—or perhaps it was more of a hope—that her would-be-murderers were on the ship meant to carry the bandits to the safety of Carthage.

How a pair of fake Egyptians could disappear without a trace was a mystery. If they were wise, the sister and brother would disappear for good.

Kadar nudged him with an oxen-sized elbow. "Have you given any thought to where you will go if today's outcome is unfavorable to Herod?"

He did not have an answer and had not heard King Herod state a plan. Conveniently for them, Rhodes was a favored outpost for political exiles. "I am betting on Herod's talent for charming Romans."

"He has been a good friend to Rome," Kadar conceded.

"And to you."

"Herod was good to me," Kadar's voice held a *but*. "Ten years can change a man. I lost a good deal of respect for him when I heard how he executed your wife's father. And his murdering John Hyrcanus was inexcusable."

James shifted on the bench's faded red cushion. "Herod will be pleased to see you. He will take your presence as a sign of support."

"I could not care less what Herod thinks." Kadar blew out a heavy breath. "If you wish or need to return to Rome, I have multiple construction projects in mind and many friends in need of a talented master builder."

Overseeing the building of warehouses, apartment buildings, and the occasional grand home could not compare to the glories of the amphitheaters, bathing complexes, and fortress castles Herod envisioned. "I appreciate the offer, but I do not care to live off of well-meaning welfare and pity."

"And some men never change." Disappointment marred Kadar's broad face.

A punch from the giant man's fist would have come as less of a blow.

He was saved from finding a reply at the stirring in the hall as King Herod and his councilors filed in. James's spineless hypocrite of a brother-in-law sat close beside Herod. The donkey-faced man refused to show kindness to Libi, but had no problem groveling at Herod's feet.

Emperor Octavian made his entrance and a deafening stillness descended. Thirty-three years of age, he had soft curly locks and pink cheeks, but there was nothing delicate or weak about his reputation. Octavian ascended the dais with the confidence one would expect of the most powerful man in the world, his position cemented by the decisive defeat of Antony and Cleopatra. With no competitors in sight, rumor said he would soon be honored with the title Caesar Augustus.

Octavian sat on his *curule* chair, which had magnificent gold filigree legs forming a large X. An aide whispered in his ear while he studied a series of documents. A lift of the emperor's finger silenced the aide, who collected the thick papyrus sheets and melted into the background.

Octavian inspected Herod with a piercing stare bound to make one's blood run cold. "What do you have to say for yourself, Herod of Idumea?"

Dressed in a royal-purple robe, Herod had wisely chosen to forgo wearing a crown. The gesture did nothing to diminish his magnetism. He rose and managed to remain a picture of calm. But James would bet his fortune the king's heart was racing as fast as his own.

"I have no wish to apologize or deny my actions." Herod's voice held no hint of servility or timidity. "I was the truest of friends to Antony."

Shock jolted the chamber. Herod had never lacked for boldness, James would say that for him.

"Continue." Octavian leaned forward.

Herod advanced to the dais. "My army was unable to fight beside Antony's as I was engaged in war with Nabatea, but I sent coins and food. Because he was my benefactor, I was obliged to assist his efforts. I am ashamed I did not do more. If you consider only my actions, I am indeed guilty."

His broad shoulders unbending, Herod spread his arm in a gesture of appeal. "But if you will trade your name for Antony's, you will find praiseworthy my loyalty and friendship to a benefactor. You can be certain I will serve you as faithfully and unwaveringly as I served Antony."

A long moment passed. Then Emperor Octavian smiled.

"I believe you will. And I will happily count you among my friends and as a friend of Rome, *King* Herod."

James stood and clapped loudly. Kadar remained seated. Herod's supporters swarmed around him, offering congratulations and praise.

"Elizabeth and Lydia will want to hear the good news," James said over the din.

"Good for who?" Kadar was grim-faced.

James smoothed his robe and plunged through the milling crowd. The victory marked the start of a new day, a new era.

With the kingship firmly in his hands, Herod was now free to redesign and renovate Israel in the image of Rome and Greece. And James would achieve his dream to be a master builder of cities and a nation.

Phaedra and Saul would meet their end if they dared showed their painted faces in Israel.

James would convince Libi to give Herod one more chance. The king was sure to turn from his deadly ways after this marvelous victory.

Elizabeth would learn to love their life in Jerusalem.

Everything was going to work out for the best. He was sure of it.

CHAPTER 34

T he day after Herod's triumph, James directed Libi to the palatial garden complex situated behind their temporary residence, a marvelous gem waiting for the loving touch of a master builder. Hiring a gardener would be a good first step.

"Why would Herod ask to meet in the maze?" Libi laughed as they weaved around the overgrown bushes framing the labyrinth at the center of the garden.

Unease licked at James's heels. "Herod promised a surprise. I was intrigued...now I am just annoyed."

Libi skipped over the grass carpet. "I ventured a short way into the maze one day while you were away but turned back for fear of becoming hopelessly lost."

"Lydia and Kadar's arrival has cheered you?"

She reached for his hand and twined her fingers with his. "Immensely. I hope Alexandra and Nathan can leave their olive farm behind for a short visit to Jerusalem. What a merry reunion that will be."

The air smelled sweeter the deeper they moved into the maze.

"Lydia and Alexandra will be giddy at reuniting."

"Admit it. You will be equally happy."

Until recently he would not have been able to agree. "I wish only that I could welcome them to the mansion home I will build for us instead of—"

"Your father's house is large enough."

The path forked again, and he went right and she went left, almost causing them to tumble to the soft grass.

Her laugh was music from the heavens. "I thought I was leading and you were following."

"I do not remember agreeing to that." He tried to frown, but grinned instead.

Taking the left path, they raced around a corner with Libi smiling triumphantly and came to an abrupt halt. A canopy of grapevines shaded the circular dead end and cast dappled sunlight over the marble table and benches where King Herod, Phaedra, and Saul were seated. Niv was pouring red wine into five ornate goblets.

All the muscles in James's body tightened.

Libi pressed close and clasped his elbow. So much for her hope the couple had sailed off to Carthage never to be seen again.

There was one comfort—Phaedra and Saul looked equally uneasy.

Fidgeting, Niv slopped wine over the table.

"Here they are." A lone island of serenity, Herod waved for them to join him. "My favorite master builder and his stoic bride."

James led Libi to a stone bench. Red droplets quivered on the polished white marble.

"Tell the truth and all will be well," she whispered in his ear as they sat.

Was she giving him permission to seek the couple's destruction? Would Herod believe his story or fall for the Egyptian's lies?

Niv dived in and wiped away the wine. He winked at James, then scurried away clutching the stained rag and the pitcher of wine.

Was Niv mocking him? James swallowed heavily. He had been a fool to trust a slave whose loyalties shifted faster than desert sand. "How good of Saul and Phaedra to finally put in an appearance." He shot a pointed look at Phaedra and Saul. "But you already paid a visit to Elizabeth."

Phaedra clasped Herod's arm. "Ask James about a harlot by the name of—"

"Shut your mouth, woman," Herod snarled. "Take your hand away before I have your arm cut off."

Phaedra recoiled, and the color drained from her narrow face.

Saul picked nervously at his goateed chin. "What lies have James Onias and my ex—"

"Do you deny hiring bandits to kill Elizabeth Onias?" Herod demanded, stone-faced.

Saul pointed at James. "He hired the bandits to kill *us*."

At Herod's derisive laugh, the songbirds exploded away from the grapevine thicket.

"Your decision to cheat the bandits out of the coins you promised was foolish. They were quite unhappy with you."

Saul paled. "They came to you?"

"Saul," Phaedra hissed. "Do not say another word."

Herod chuckled. "I agree. Elizabeth shall have the last say." He turned to Libi. "I cannot rectify the past, but I am anxious to mend ways with you. I leave the fate of Saul and Phaedra in your hands. Do you wish to see them executed or banished?"

"Elizabeth," Phaedra cried and pushed her hair away

from her face. "Do not abandon us. We took you in, a *zavah* woman, when nobody else wanted you. And we showed you many other kindnesses."

Libi sent the older woman a pained look. "I am and was grateful. And have repeatedly begged my husband to extend mercy on you."

Saul scrambled off his seat and fell on his knees before Libi. "Please spare our lives."

"James, you must decide. I cannot." Her expression anguished, Libi clasped James's hand.

Saul walked on his knees to James. "I do not want to be a master builder. I want to live."

"You and your wife will be safer if the Boethus siblings are dead," Herod said conversationally, sipping wine from one of the untouched goblets.

Niv must not have told the king about the couple's alliance with Cleopatra and their poison plan.

Hanging on James's decision, Phaedra and Saul appeared as old and worn as their makeup.

Why couldn't he send them to a deserved death?

Because Libi would blame herself.

"We choose banishment." He squeezed her fingers.

He felt a tremble go through her.

Saul collapsed, weeping.

"Where will we go?" Phaedra asked, glassy-eyed.

Herod climbed to his feet. "Carthage would be a good start. If you ever try to return to Egypt or Israel, you will be executed. Do I make myself clear?"

"We will be on the next ship bound for the far side of the Great Sea." She stooped beside her brother and patted his back.

Libi kept her head held high. "Shall we proceed to a more pleasant spot? The rose garden is quite lovely."

Herod nodded. "Your wife does you proud, James Onias."

"She certainly does." The praise felt faint. "I hope her sense of direction is better than mine or hours might pass before we reach the rose garden."

Herod laughed. "That is a problem easily solved. Follow me." He directed them through a hidden vine-covered gate.

James did not spare a backward glance for Phaedra and Saul. And neither did Libi as the gate swung closed behind her.

Herod clapped James on the back. "It seems you will be my master builder."

"Happy day, Husband." Libi hugged James. "The answer to all your dreams and hopes."

But James felt none of the expected joy.

"I need a Jewish master builder." Herod's smile lost some of its friendliness. His eyes shifted to Libi. "I expect you to help me to convince your husband to return to the priesthood." He strode away without waiting for an answer.

"I promise not to nag you to return to the priesthood." Libi's face was clouded.

Unaccountably sad instead of relieved, he feigned cheer.

"You must be eager to return to Jerusalem and worship at the Temple. I know it has been one of your dearest desires."

"Not exactly. Perhaps more anxious than eager. Andrew might cause a scene. Or the Levite guard could turn me away."

"Kadar will make sure that does not happen." James detested the idea of relying on anyone, even his brother-in-law, to protect Libi. What other choice did he have?

Libi bowed her head. "I wish…"

"I know." He hated himself right now.

CHAPTER 35

King Herod's return to Jerusalem should be a triumphant occasion, but the buzz of activity in the palace was more chaotic than joyous. Summoned to the throne room, Avda threaded his way through the flurry of servants attending to the king's guests.

Royal advisers and military men of all stripes were in attendance. Merchants, priests, and foreign dignitaries milled around the edge of the vast chamber in hopes of requesting and receiving favors. Musicians tuned their instruments at the front of the room.

Herod was in the middle of the throng, handing out gifts to his children, who romped and exclaimed at his feet.

"Physician Hama, where have you been hiding?" he called when his gaze fell on Avda.

Avda and his sons, along with Queen Mariamne's entire household, had departed Fortress Alexandrium as soon as receiving the summons to return to Jerusalem, and arrived at the palace a few hours ago.

"I was in my treatment room, checking on supplies."

Herod frowned. "What has you looking so glum? I

thought you would be sharing in my jubilation."

The king would not be pleased when he learned Avda would be leaving his position as physician to the royal household. He would wait to deliver the news in private and not detract from Herod's victory.

"Please accept my sincere felicitations."

But the king was distracted by a slave whispering in his ear. Herod's face turned deep red at the message.

"She refused a second invitation?" he bellowed. "Tell the queen it is the king's command."

The rattled slave hurried away.

Cypros and Salome, who had been recalled from Masada, sat to Herod's left. Undoubtedly up to some new mischief, mother and daughter looked quite pleased with themselves.

Avda resisted the temptation to ask about Kitra and Jazmine's whereabouts. He had thought of them nonstop since ordering her and Taj away. The trio had not rejoined Cypros at Masada. That much he knew.

At the queen's entrance, a hush fell over the hall. Cypros and Salome's faces soured. The children, paying no mind, continued with their play.

Herod brightened. "Let the celebration begin."

A cheer went up.

"Rejoice with me, my queen," Herod said in a cajoling voice.

Mariamne sat without looking at her husband.

Cypros waved Avda forward.

He approached, dreading to hear the long list of current maladies afflicting his most demanding patient. With such an attitude, he knew it truly was time to move on. The last thing he wanted was to become an uncaring physician who resented those he attended to.

"Hell and crucifixion, woman," Herod growled in response to something Mariamne said. "You are still brooding?"

"You are a brute." Contempt burned in the queen's eyes. "Threatening me. Ordering my execution if the emperor did not allow you to return to the throne. Do you deny it?"

"My great love for you drives me to extremes."

"Love? You are a hypocrite. You never loved me."

Herod reared back as though snake-bit. "What is this accusation?"

"My greatest hope was that Emperor Octavian would order your execution." She balled her hands.

Gasps resounded through the chamber. The couple's two youngest children burst into tears. The older two, worried expressions pinching their faces, stared at their angry parents.

Avda groaned. Herod normally overlooked the queen's insolent attitude, due to his great affection for her. But her wish for his death bordered on reckless. And Herod was not an ordinary man, but a king. The comment could be construed as treason.

Herod pointed to an arched entryway. "Get out of my sight, Wife, before you tempt me to rashness."

Pale of face, the queen rose slowly, head high, and gathered her skirts around her with great dignity. "Come, children."

"The children will remain with me," Herod said coldly.

She winced, but recovering quickly, walked through the hushed throng with straight shoulders.

The children cried for their mother.

The pitiful wails tore at Avda's heart.

Cypros directed the numerous young nieces who attended her to comfort and distract their young cousins.

A pall hung over the room.

Bony-armed Salome smiled with relish.

Her glee disgusted Avda. He searched for words to calm Herod. "Her Highness's displeasure is understandable."

The king turned on him. "Did you share our private conversation with my wife?"

Avda swallowed. How to diffuse Herod's suspicion without implicating Sohemus? Not that the fool deserved help after disregarding Avda's advice to keep his mouth closed.

"I have never betrayed your trust, and never will."

Herod blew out a weary breath and scrubbed his woolly beard. "Forgive me. I let my temper take over."

It was growing more difficult to hang onto the hope Herod would gain a measure of peace and happiness, despite the ever upward trajectory of victories won, armies and wealth amassed, and titles and stature attained.

"A soft word turns away wrath, but grievous words stir up anger." Avda quoted King Solomon, a man far wiser than himself.

Seemingly chastened, Herod's shoulders fell.

"Would you talk to her? She might listen to you."

From all Mariamne had confided to him and Sohemus of her indignation and disgust with her husband, she might have been pushed past the point of forgiveness.

"I can try."

Salome smirked and drummed her fingers on the arms of her carved-wood chair. "Physician Hama, word reached us at Masada, saying Sohemus and Queen Mariamne had grown quite close. Did you witness any inappropriate behavior?"

"The adulterous whore," Herod bawled.

Avda's veins iced. He was beginning to hate the sight of the conniving woman.

"You are *again* guilty of spreading false rumors."

"I will strangle her if it is true." Herod shook with anger.

Avda was not the only one mortified, judging by the stricken faces throughout the room. Given John Hyrcanus's recent fate and that of Herod's uncle under the same circumstances, the threat could not be dismissed.

Salome's vulture eyes fixed on Avda. "Physician Hama, you would be wise not to forget where your loyalty rests."

Ori and Benjamin came before anybody and anything.

"Are you accusing me of being a traitor?"

She clucked her tongue, but the viciousness did not vanish from her sharp face. "There is no need to be testy."

Herod paused from his pacing and beckoned to Niv.

"Find Sohemus and order him to meet me in my private chamber."

If Sohemus was prudent, he would guard his words. Especially while this jealous mood ruled the king.

Cypros rubbed her temple. "Physician Hama, my head is about to bursts. I need you to fix one of your cures immediately."

Avda respectfully bowed his head. "I will return shortly."

Despite her imperiousness, he respected her devotion to her son and daughter. He would make this last cure for her Grandness, then inform the king he and the boys were leaving the palace and the country.

For good.

CHAPTER 36

J ames entered the palace reception chamber with due
caution. Word had it King Herod was in a ferocious
mood due to the queen's refusal to resume marital relations. She was angry at Herod ordering her death if the
trial had gone badly.

The information had come the usual way—from palace slaves, to a chain of household slaves, to his slaves.
Saad and Marcus had relished sharing all the salacious
details.

James's sympathy rested with the queen.

Kadar had insisted on accompanying him to the palace, most likely at Lydia's behest. He welcomed his
brother-in-law's sound judgment and formidable presence.

The spacious hall buzzed with activity as the usual
guests and extended family members vied for the king's
attention.

Sprawled on a purple cushioned couch, Herod wore a
distracted brooding face as his mother and sister yam-
mered in his ears.

Out of the corner of an eye, James saw a red head.

Niv scurried across the room, clutching a giant silver

goblet.

"The rat comes out of his hole," James mumbled. It had been just a matter of time before he caught up with the traitor.

Niv did not look left or right, but went straight to King Herod, and bowed. "Queen Mariamne sends a gift."

Face brightening, Herod sat up and held out his hands for the goblet. "Did she?"

"The wine is laced with a love potion." Niv hugged the silver cup to his breast.

"Love potion." Herod exploded off the couch.

Eyes huge as boulders, Niv nodded.

"For what purpose?" Herod paced. "The witch, inflaming my passions as she continues to spurn my attentions."

Niv's freckles stood out on his pale face. "The queen did not inform me of her intentions. I did warn her that too large a dose of the potion could be deadly."

"My wife wants to murder me?" Disbelief and anger warred on Herod's face.

James's nose for lies stinking of bull dung had him doubting every word Niv had spoken. What was the fool slave doing getting caught up in another deadly scheme? He was fortunate to have kept his head on his shoulders after delivering the poison that had sent Herod's father to the grave.

"Your queen seems to have grown tired of you," Salome purred.

It was a good bet she was the one who had put Niv up to this treachery against the queen.

Herod eyes remained wild. "Whoever turned Mariamne against me is a dead man."

"Perhaps Sohemus could enlighten us." Salome's sweet

smile would sicken a roomful of healthy people.

The knot of royal advisers gathered in the corner shuffled aside until a man in a urine-colored tunic was left standing alone.

Herod glowered at the man. "Did my wife play the whore with you while I was in Rhodes?"

Sohemus' face turned a shade of ugly green. "I swear nothing untoward happened."

"I do not believe you," Herod bellowed.

"I am innocent." Sohemus swayed on his feet. "This is a wicked trick."

"Trick?" Salome snickered. "The queen is the one who tried to lure the king with a love potion."

Herod snapped his fingers at his head guardsman.

"Arrest him. Place guards outside the queen's bed-chamber and assemble all her slaves for questioning. I will learn the truth, by God, if I have to torture them all—down to her young maidens."

An uproar erupted in the chamber.

"Out!" Herod ordered. "Everyone get out."

James's stomach sickened. "Those poor creatures. What can be done to save them?"

"He will not listen to anyone right now." Kadar gripped his shoulder.

James searched the room, but Niv had already escaped. He ground his teeth. "Anyone except Salome. The fiend-ish woman does not have one speck of compassion in her bony body."

Kadar had taken on the look of a warrior prepared for battle. "We should return to the women and children."

For good reason. All of Jerusalem would be on edge until Herod's rage passed.

CHAPTER 37

How many times had Avda stood at this bench using mortar and pestle to crush herbs, with the boys seated at the dining table reciting scriptures or telling stories or squabbling over minor matters?

Concocting a cure for Cypros's headache was a simple task compared to explaining to his sons why they would be leaving to start a new life in a distant land. Next would come the unpleasant job of informing Herod and Cypros of his plans.

Pounding on the door interrupted his thoughts.

Ori hurried across the room.

The knocking turned to multiple thuds. "Open the door," several deep voices demanded.

Ori wrenched open the door and four Idumean guardsmen barged in.

"Come with us, Avda Hama," the lead man growled.

Ori's face puckered. "What do you want with Father?"

They ignored the boy.

Benjamin hurried to Avda and clung to his arm. "Tell them to go away."

He patted his son's head. Herod in a stormy mood was

nothing he hadn't dealt with before. The presence of the guardsmen was troubling.

"Go back to your schoolwork, boys. I will return shortly."

Leaving the apartment behind, he turned in the direction of the reception chamber.

A guardsman grabbed his shoulder, pulling him to a stop. The brute hitched his thumb over his shoulder. "Wrong way, prisoner Hama."

Avda's blood ran cold. "Prisoner? You are taking me to the basement chambers? There must be a mistake."

The man shrugged. "I have my orders."

Avda braced his feet and fisted his hands. His sons would be alone and defenseless without him. "I demand to speak to Herod."

The closest guardsman shoved him. "Get moving."

Avda stumbled but managed to remain on his feet. "Keep your hands to—"

"Leave Father alone," Ori shouted from the doorway.

"Father?" Tears flowed down Benjamin's white face.

Rage and fear coursing through his veins, Avda struggled to keep his voice steady. "There has been a mistake. Ori, watch after your brother until I return. Benjamin, listen to your brother."

"You can count on us, Father." Ori put an arm around his younger brother.

He had never been prouder of his sons. Or more afraid for them.

Avda sat on his haunches at the back of a pitch-black cell that smelled of sweat, urine, and terror. A day and a night had passed without a word from the outside world or a reason given for his arrest.

His sons must be worried sick. He prayed they were safe and well. Surely Herod would not stoop so low as to punish or harm innocent children. But who would believe he would be treating a lifelong friend and ally so abominably? A new thought destroyed him.

The blame did not rest completely on Herod. *He* shared culpability. The murder of High Priest Hyrcanus was a clue to the instability of Herod's mind. He should have taken the boys and fled far from the king and Israel.

A chill invaded bone deep.

The hesitation could prove costly, or perhaps deadly.

Why had he stayed?

Kitra, in all her vitality and loveliness, filled his vision.

Would he see her again?

If, no, *when* he escaped this cell, he would do everything differently. Especially where Kitra was concerned.

His gut clenched as the next series of pitiful screams pierced the hellish prison. Who was being tortured? Would he be next?

He covered his ear. Herod would never have him tortured. Or would he?

Many hours later, the cell door scraped open, waking him from a fitful sleep.

He lumbered to his feet and squinted against the brightness of a burning torch. He was prepared to beg, bribe, or lie his way to freedom. "Who's there?"

The tinkling of bracelets and the faint scent of exotic perfume gave him his answer. His heart leaped. "Kitra, it is too dangerous. You should not be here."

She rushed to him and wrapped her slender yet strong arm around his and tugged him toward the door. "We must hurry."

CHAPTER 38

After the half-day flight on horseback from Jerusalem to nearby Idumea, Kitra did not dare celebrate as she and Jazmine helped Avda, Ori, and Benjamin settle into the largest guest tent the family compound boasted. Luxuriously carpeted and furnished, it was closer to a palace room than a goat herder's simple dwelling. "When you have eaten, bathed, and rested, my father wishes to meet with you."

Overjoyed to see the boys, Jazmine bounced on tiptoes and chirped away, pointing to the fresh tunics in many colors and bowls overflowing with fruits, nuts, and bread.

Avda touched Kitra's arm. Though dusty and weary, his kind brown eyes were filled with luminous warmth. "Is this real? Are you real? I fear I will wake any moment to find last night and today are a dream."

She laughed so she would not cry. "Or more like a nightmare? The Jewish Physician Hama as a guest of the idol-worshiper Faakhir Aretas."

He frowned and moved closer. "I count it an honor." His warm breath caressed her ear. "I hate that you put yourself in so much danger."

His quiet strength and reassuring presence always soothed. "Your boys deserve the praise. I went to you as soon as their letter arrived informing me of your arrest."

He stroked her arms. His hands, beautiful hands used to heal others, but now chapped and calloused, were rough on her skin. "They are brave boys, wise to seek your capable help."

She had not felt brave or capable. "I begged and begged Aunt Cypros to plead your case, but I do not know if the king would have agreed to release you if Mariamne's eunuch slave had not finally broken under torture."

Avda looked pained. "I heard the poor man's cries."

The thought of Avda being maimed or hurt had haunted her on the breakneck journey from Idumea to Jerusalem.

"The eunuch confessed that he had witnessed Sohemus often in the queen's company. And my cousin the king took it as proof of an affair between Sohemus and Queen Mariamne."

"And Sohemus paid for his indiscretion with his life." Grief edged Avda's soft voice. "And the queen is to stand trial for adultery and attempted murder?"

Sohemus had been executed and the queen placed under house arrest shortly before Kitra arrived at the Palace. Her aunt Cypros and cousin Salome had joyfully shared the whole story.

Renewed guilt washed through her over the shameful attempt to steal Herod away from Mariamne. Just because she had never cared for Mariamne did not mean she wanted to see her put to death.

She glanced toward Jazmine, who sat in a corner of the tent on a pile of plush cushions and was chattering away to Ori and Benjamin. Although others felt no such reservation, she mourned the thought of Herod's four young children left motherless.

"Cypros and Salome will not stop until they are permanently rid of Mariamne."

Avda's hands tightened on her arms. "I am ashamed of my misplaced loyalty to the king and his family. It is a mistake I will not repeat."

She heard echoes of her father and brother's voices instructing her to use her seductive powers to gain Avda's cooperation. Her flirtatious tricks had never worked on him. "Please tell me the vow does not include me."

Strong arms pulled her into an embrace. "You own my heart."

Would that be true after he learned the truth? "Father wishes us to marry. It is the reason he welcomed you here."

"Why? What could he possibly hope to gain from the marriage."

"To save his favorite son...Taj." Wretchedness tightened her throat.

Avda's eyes softened. "I will not tell Herod of Taj's attempts to seduce Queen Mariamne if that is what your father fears. But not for their sake, but for yours."

"I am afraid for you." Awed by his tender care, she pressed closer.

He frowned. "Why?"

She traced a finger over his solid chest. "Father says torture breaks the strongest of men and women, and they will confess to almost anything. If Herod changes his mind over releasing you..." The tang of vomit welled in her mouth. "Surely, Herod would not subject you to torture."

"The Herod I knew in my youth, no. But the man he has

become…" A distant look filled his eyes, and he exhaled heavily. "I had been waiting for the right time to inform Herod I planned to leave his service and this part of the world. Rome has a large Jewish population." His brow furrowed. "Is it too much to ask you to join me?"

Life with Avda would be beautiful and happy, but not without obstacles. "I know I am nothing like your other wives, but—"

"I do not have riches," he said without apology. "I cannot provide you with the costly clothes and jewels and the palace homes you are accustomed to."

Life as a physician's wife represented a sea change. "I understand your doubts because I have the same ones. But I know this…" She jingled her pretty bracelets and shook her mane of black hair. "When my beauty fades and I am an old woman, you will still love and treasure me."

"I will cherish you all the more." Love shone in his eyes.

"And that is priceless."

"Kiss Mama," Jazmine exclaimed. "Mama wants you to kiss her, don't you?"

She and Avda shared a laugh. The boys grinned too.

Avda pecked her cheek. "Will that do?"

Jazmine clapped, then returned to playing with her favorite doll.

Ori and Benjamin smiled broadly and politely turned away to give their father privacy.

Kitra already loved them.

"They are good boys. They will make wonderful big brothers."

Avda's arm circled her in a tender embrace. "They adore Jazmine. And you."

"Father and Taj will be surprised and relieved that you quickly agreed to marry me."

He held her at arm's length and his brown eyes held a fierce glint.

"Your father and Taj are welcome to go to hell. I am marrying you because I want to. Because I love you and cannot live without you."

Her heart thrilled at the adamant declaration. "I love you more than words can say, Avda Hama."

His kiss took away her breath.

"Take me to your father," he said, drawing in a deep breath of his own.

Jazmine giggled. Ori and Benjamin clapped and whistled approvingly.

She bit her lip, anticipating their wedding night. "I have a great favor to ask when you settle the terms of the marriage."

He stroked her back. "Whatever is your pleasure."

"You might not feel the same when you hear the request."

"My curiosity is increasing."

She swallowed. "I want my mother freed from her desert prison and to have her come live with us in Rome. I must warn you, she can be a difficult woman."

Avda smiled. "Years of dealing with her sister, her Grandness Cypros, has me well prepared."

Relief and joy tumbled through her. "I do not deserve you."

"I am no saint." He kissed her brow.

"No?" Avda Hama would be the last person she would expect of holding deep dark secrets.

"I snore."

She laughed, but the reprieve was brief. "We have to

act swiftly. In case Herod has a change of heart."

"I can only imagine how opulent your father's tent must be."

Avda's suite of rooms, smelling of herbs and ointment, had always felt cozy and welcoming.

"For all the wealth my father has, he is none the happier for it."

She led him outside and into the arms of a glorious desert sunset.

CHAPTER 39

A day after negotiating a highly favorable marriage contract with Faakhir Aretas, Avda wed Kitra in a Jewish ceremony in the middle of her family's idol-worshiping compound.

A lavish wedding feast proceeded with remarkable gaiety and goodwill. The grandiosity of his father-in-law's central tent and furnishings exceeded expectations and proved the man placed a high priority on "showing off his wealth."

A slave delivered another gift from Kitra's stepmother—two magnificent silver wine goblets. "I thought she and your stepsisters despised you," Avda whispered in Kitra's ear as he acknowledged the gift with a smile and a nod.

Kitra's beauty outshined her bejeweled stepsisters all the more for her choice of a modest gown.

"They are happy to be rid of me as Father favored me above any of his wife's daughters."

"I hope you will continue to wear your bangles. I am partial to their musical chime." He touched the single bracelet circling her slender wrist.

Her exotic almond eyes lit with joy. "I would miss them."

"Would you want me to start wearing costly colorful robes and gold rings on my fingers?"

She laughed. "Oh my, no."

"Well, I love you as you are."

"How could I not fall in love with you?" She kissed his cheek.

The enticing smell of her perfume was a punch to the gut. "How are we to spend our riches thanks to your father's generous wedding present if you do not purchase lovely gowns and beautiful baubles?"

"You mean the generous *bribe*."

He had sworn an oath to remain silent about Taj's plan to seduce Queen Mariamne, but his word of honor had not been good enough. "If throwing riches at me makes your father feel more secure, who was I to argue?" Refusing the gift would have been short-sighted and spiteful.

Her eyes clouded, and she bit her lower lip. "Father is unaware of the depth of your sacrifice."

Taj's poisonous affair with Chaya had been a festering wound. But sitting in a dark cell, staring torture or death in the face had focused Avda on what mattered most.

"The past is in the past. Ori, Benjamin, Jazmine, and you are all I hold important."

Tears shone in her eyes. "My love for Taj feels like a betrayal."

"He is your brother. I would never ask you to deny what is in your heart."

Her trembling hand cupped his cheek. "Bless you, Husband."

Jazmine raced to them and crawled onto her mother's lap. Her sweet face was hidden behind a mask of pink rouge and lip paint. A glittery band circled her up-swept hair. Her gown was more suitable for a harlot than a four-year-old. "Do you like my pretty clothes and hair?"

"I have missed you, my darling." Kitra sent a sharp look at her father and stepmother, who were responsible for the shameful attire and makeup.

A grasping woman, her stepmother was busy coaxing her oldest daughter toward a wealthy arms dealer who looked three times older than the poor girl.

Faakhir parted company with his sons and strolled over to their table.

"Kitra, why are you not smiling, my beautiful dove?"

Kitra hugged Jazmine. "She is still a baby."

"My wife says it is best to teach them at a young age." Faakhir reached out to Jazmine. "Come and dazzle the boys, my little dove, the way Haabeel taught you. Your mother must attend to her husband."

"Why do I have to smile at them?" Jazmine shrank back against her mother. "They are always mean and laugh when I cry."

"Tell Haabeel her help and advice are not wanted," Kitra said.

Distaste showed on her father's elegant face. "What use are daughters except for capturing prized husbands?"

Kitra hugged Jazmine with motherly ferocity. "She is more precious to me than gold or gems."

Faakhir wrinkled his nose. "Do not burden your new husband with another man's daughter. I could easily strike a bargain with a Nabatean prince eager to make an advantageous match for his ten-year-old son. The actual marriage would not—"

Disgusted, Avda intervened. "Leave Jazmine's welfare to us."

Kitra hiked her chin. "Avda loves Jazmine."

"Father Avda loves me," Jazmine echoed sweetly, and

lifted her little chin like her mother.

It was the first time she had called him father. Avda's heart swelled.

"I am blessed to have such a precious daughter."

Jazmine giggled and jumped off her mother's lap. "I see Ori and Benjamin," she exclaimed and skipped off.

"Good luck controlling your tart-mouthed women." His father-in-law's mouth twisted with a derisive smirk.

"I have no wish to control them," Avda replied.

Faakhir shook his head and retreated to his sons.

Kitra slumped against his shoulder. "From the time I was a little girl I worked to please him."

Distaste for his contemptible father-in-law reached new heights. Avda stroked her slender back.

"After our move to Rome, you will probably never see your father again. Does that make you sad?"

"Do you think he will miss me?" She sighed. "I can see now nothing I did would ever be enough because I was not one of his beloved sons. But we can save Jazmine from the same pain."

Taj sauntered up. "Sister, since when did you become so tenderhearted?"

"What do you want?" Avda glared up at Kitra's brother.

"Leave." Kitra sat up straight. "You are not welcome here."

Taj's sly smile vanished. "Would you be so cruel as to deny me the opportunity to wish you a happy marriage?"

Avda's sympathy rested with Kitra. Given her love for her brother, this had to be difficult for her.

"You do not have to forsake your brother on my account."

Kitra pointed to the closest exit. "Go."

Taj frowned. "I wrote to Mother saying Sabina and I

would come to Rome to visit her. Mother always liked my wife."

"Arrange to meet her anywhere in Rome you like, for as long as you like," Kitra said calmly. "But you will never be allowed to enter our home."

Taj shot a nasty look at Avda. "Write me when you tire of your boring husband." Then he strode to his father and brothers."

"I will ask father to have him removed." Kitra turned to Avda, and her eyes held an apology.

"Why? You set him in his place."

The lines of tension on her face smoothed. "I did."

"I meant what I said. I do not expect you to forsake your family."

"My loyalty belongs to you."

"Taj seems quite sure you will grow bored with me."

"Umm.... No. Never." Gold-flecked fingernails caressed his jaw.

He kissed her palm. "I sense this is the start of a wonderful adventure."

The thunder of horse hooves sounded beyond the tent walls.

Avda frowned. "Were you expecting more guests?"

"No."

A moment later, soldiers barged into the tent. King Herod rumbled in behind them.

"Avda Hama! You have much to answer to."

Silence descended, and the wedding guests bowed low.

Avda jumped to his feet and shielded Kitra.

"What is the charge?"

"How dare you marry without inviting me?" Herod braced his hands on his hips and glowered darkly.

Avda blinked, not sure if he had heard correctly.

Herod threw back his head in laughter. "You should see your face."

"Infernal flames," Avda swore. "Did you have to put the fear of Satan in everyone? And, no, you were not invited to the wedding. And, yes, it was on purpose."

Faakhir hustled to Herod. "We are honored by your presence."

Merriment undeterred, Herod tossed a coin bag at Avda. "Your wedding present."

Avda caught the surprisingly heavy bag and handed it to Kitra. After years of being at the family's constant call, he reckoned he had earned it.

"This will not make me forget your unjust treatment."

Gasps arose.

"You are speaking to the king," Faakhir reminded him.

Herod dipped his head, then looked up in contrition. "Your arrest was a mistake."

"Mistake?"

"You know how upset Mariamne can make me."

Though his repentance was sincere enough, Avda knew it would last only until the next time something set the unstable man off. Asking what Herod hoped to accomplish by arresting him was a waste of time.

He cleared his dry throat. "You received my letter resigning my post as palace physician?"

"Please tell me you will return to Jerusalem." Herod closed the distance between them. "My mother is inconsolable over the news."

Avda wondered how different matters might have turned out if Herod's father and brothers had lived.

"I will send over detailed notes on the composition of your mother's favored cures for the next physician."

"There must be a way to mend matters," Herod

pressed.

"Not this time."

The king's shoulders fell. "This is our final parting then?"

Avda should have left years ago, but he had continued to hope the great potential he'd seen in his friend would overcome the faults. The opposite had happened.

"Give my kindest regards to your mother."

Herod winked at Kitra. "Do you have a farewell hug for your favorite cousin?"

"Of course." She gave him a quick embrace.

"I do believe my cousin is smitten with you," Herod said with an approving smile.

Faakhir waved one of his younger daughters forward. "May I introduce Dara for your pleasure?"

In the flower of her youth at sixteen, Dara sashayed to Herod's side. "My Lord and King," she said in a sultry voice.

Herod laughed at the young woman. "You must be one of Faakhir's squadron of temptresses."

Kitra's father snapped his fingers at the girl, dismissing her.

Dara fled and sobbed on her mother's breast.

Herod met Avda's eye. "If your father-in-law treats you poorly I want to know."

Faakhir and Taj stared nervously at Herod and Avda. With King Herod in an executing mood over Queen Mariamne, Taj had very good reason to worry.

Avda must tread close to the dangerous subject. "Please free the queen. She has done nothing wrong."

"Happy marriage, Physician Hama and Cousin Kitra." Herod's gaze frosted over, he turned and strode out of the tent and the soldiers followed closely on his heels.

Kitra pressed closer to Avda. "Can we do anything for Mariamne?"

Distress for the queen and her children weighed heavily. "I am afraid she is at Herod's mercy."

"The poor woman." Kitra shivered.

The confines of the tent even more oppressive, Avda clasped her hand. "Come away with me." And he whisked her out a side entrance.

The sun blazed bright on the sleeping countryside. Horses grazed the hills under an endless blue sky. The flowers of the field he favored for curing fevers flourished among the tall windswept grasses.

He drew her under the protective branches of an ancient terebinth tree. "Will you miss Idumea?"

"Our new life in Rome will be heavenly." Love glowed in her almond-shaped eyes.

"You feel it too?" He smiled and kissed her beautiful hands. "That all will be well as long as we are together as a family?"

He was rewarded with the loveliest of smiles. "I do. Marrying for true love was a foreign notion. Your love is the most precious gift imaginable. I will cherish it always."

"I am renewed in heart and soul and body since the day you reentered my life." He kissed her tenderly.

They shared a smiled as Ori and Benjamin walked toward them holding Jazmine's hands and joined them under the terebinth tree.

Avda's heart sang with a new song, and he glanced heavenward.

Surely goodness and mercy shall follow me all the days of my life.

CHAPTER 40

One week after his ex-wife had married Physician Hama, James was an attendee to Queen Mariamne's trial for adultery and attempted murder. He stood at the back of the Hall of Hewn Stone. The traitorous rat Niv was putting on a performance worthy of a Greek actor, accusing the queen of attempting to poison King Herod.

Seated in the royal box, Herod had armored himself in anger as his sister Salome glared vulture-like across the chamber at Mariamne. The queen remained a picture of regal composure, but not so her mother. If Aalexis beat the air any faster with her plumed fan, she would whip up a thunderstorm.

James surveyed the gray uninspiring sanctuary. The last time he had darkened the meeting place of the Sanhedrin, he had been the one on trial. The irony was too rich not to be enjoyed. If named as master builder he would oversee the reconstruction of the Temple complex, including this hall. The drawings of Herod's planned replacement would enshrine the High Priest and other Temple leaders in a glorious structure. Thanks to James.

The ghost of his father's voice invaded his musings. *You are a disgrace.*

James's trial had ended with his father slapping him across the face. He pressed his hand to his cheek. The sting of the blow had quickly faded, but not so the shame. Public humiliation and the years of abuse pushed James beyond pure hatred to plotting patricide.

It happened that the young slave Niv knew where to secretly attain poison.

James snagged Niv's plump arm as he scurried for the exit. "You cannot hide from me forever," he said, amid the audience moving about and buzzing with gossip as the next witness was called.

Niv's eyes widened. "Salome will not look kindly on you mistreating me."

"Let me guess. The enticement to become Phaedra's next husband paled in comparison to the bribe Salome offered?"

"Salome offered me my freedom and promised to find a place for me in the army. I will finally be a soldier."

The young slave's determination to escape his miserable lot in life was admirable if inconvenient.

"Good for you." James shot back. Niv wouldn't mistake his sarcastic tone.

Several young priests—men who had been young brats when James had discarded his heritage and walked away from the priesthood—gave them dirty looks for being too loud.

He tugged Niv closer. "Do you care that turning on me to scheme with Phaedra and Saul almost got my wife killed?"

"What did you expect?" Niv whispered harshly. "You have been holding my past over my head for years. Forcing me to spy for you."

The truth was hard to argue with. "So the dog turns on the master?"

"I am not your dog or anybody else's." Niv broke free of his grasp.

"Salome might feel differently."

"I am using her. Just as I used you to get what I wanted."

James winced. He had underestimated Niv.

The alliance he and Elizabeth had made with Phaedra and Saul would look suspicious on the surface. Given the unbalanced state of Herod's mind, nobody was safe.

He used the one weapon at his disposal—the threat of exposing Niv's part in Antipater's death. "I swear on Elizabeth's life, your secret is safe with me."

Niv arched a brow. "An olive branch from James Onias? What do you want in return?"

"A truce. You go your way...I go mine."

Niv chuckled. "You expect me to believe that?"

"Salome will not be able to save you if I spill my secret," James replied through gnashed teeth.

An unrepentant grin spread across Niv's freckled face. "How will you explain away your years of silence?" Not waiting for a reply, the slave and would-be-soldier scurried for the hall's double doors.

The traitorous rat must die. And soon.

James cringed. Where had that come from?

To murder Niv would make him no better than Phaedra or Salome or...his father.

Forgive me, he prayed, bowing his head.

The trio of presiding judges stood to pronounce the verdict in this farce of a trial. Herod had proclaimed he believed his wife guilty and the judges would have to be brave indeed to defy the king. Past familiarity with the men involved left no doubt as to the path they would take.

"Guilty," came the first voice.

The next two judges likewise refused to look up as they mumbled their own pronouncements of guilt.

"We hereby pass a sentence of death on Mariamne Hasmonean," the first judge continued ashen-faced.

A loud murmur swept the hall and a visible tremble went through Herod. Salome wore a satisfied sneer as she patted Herod's back in a consoling manner. The Hasmonean loyalists were clearly shaken, whereas the Herodians did nothing to hide their delight.

James was gutted by the decision, despite expecting it. Just because he had no love for the Hasmoneans did not mean he wished to see one of the few remaining members of the storied family executed.

Queen Mariamne alone remained a picture of calm and grace.

The first judge raised his voice over the stir. "We find Mariamne guilty of adultery and attempted murder of the king. However..."

Herod's shoulders tightened, and he leaned forward.

Features drawn and knuckles white on the arms of his chair, the judge cleared his throat. "In the event evidence arises exonerating the queen, we recommend the execution be delayed and that the queen be imprisoned in one of the kingdom's desert fortresses."

"Delayed," Herod repeated, visibly wavering.

Salome whispered in his ear.

Shaking her off, he stood. "Very well. I order the queen to be removed to—

"My wicked daughter is undeserving of your benevolent mercy," Aalexis cried, hopping to her feet.

Herod looked toward Aalexis and Mariamne for the first time.

Aalexis threw her plumed fan at Mariamne. "I begged my daughter over and over not to demean and speak hatefully to you."

The queen did not flinch as the fan bounced harmlessly to the floor.

"She is a mean-minded, ungrateful woman," her mother screeched.

Contempt showed in Herod's eyes. He ought to thank the woman for the shameful display that managed to outdo his indecency.

The armed guard marched to the bench holding the women.

Aalexis tore at her graying hair. "My daughter deserves no mercy. Her punishment is well deserved."

The guards dragged the mother away kicking and screaming.

Queen Mariamne followed the guardsmen with a straight back and head held high.

Somberness engulfed the chamber. Herod and his followers slipped out a side entrance and the audience shuffled out the rear doors.

Disgusted with Aalexis and Herod, James shook his head.

Why couldn't Herod pour his passion into his grand building projects instead of this unstable obsession over his wife's fidelity?

"You are the spit and image of your father," James's elderly neighbor said, shuffling up to James with the aid of his grandsons.

James scrubbed his close-clipped hair. Poor old Jachim was more senile than ever. "I do not have a beard or his sour eyes or his mean mouth."

Wobbling in place, Jachim pointed. "Your father used to smooth his robe in the same indignant manner."

Heat flooded his face. He fisted his hands behind his back. Simeon Onias thought nothing of committing evil as he grasped after the office of High Priest. James was nothing like him. Nothing at all.

"You make an ugly Roman," Banna teased good-naturedly. "Would you ever consider returning to the fold of the priesthood?"

Benjamin pushed his stringy hair away from his lanky face. "We miss you, despite your grumpiness."

"It was the one way to hurt my father," James confessed.

Sadness dimmed the old man's eyes. "Simeon has been dead a long time now."

The insight hit home. By blaming his father, he was avoiding accepting responsibility for his choices. His own hate was keeping him from returning to his faith and heritage. Not his dead father.

"King Herod has been nagging me to denounce idol worship and return to my rightful duties," he mumbled.

"Ah yes, our *valiant* king," Banna said, a sour expression wrinkling his nose.

"By all means, beware of disappointing the king." Benjamin's lips were pursed.

Jachim beckoned James to lean down to allow him to speak into his ear.

"Stop looking back. Make your decisions with Elizabeth in mind. Make her your guiding beacon."

The last of the shackles fell away.

Beautiful, strong, loving Libi. She was the key. *His* key.

"The Lord bless you, Jachim," he said and took off at a

run.

"Where are you rushing off to?" Banna called out.

"Home," James shouted. "I am going home."

CHAPTER 41

L eaving the Hall of Hewn Stones behind, James could not get back to the house and Elizabeth fast enough. He burst into the dining chamber, startling Libi, Saad, and Marcus.

The two slaves hid their plates under their napkins and came to their feet.

Libi's brow furrowed. "You were late for the midday meal, so I invited Saad and Marcus to join me. You know how I hate to eat alone."

Curled up on a chair bathed in sunshine, Apollo rose and stretched in a lazy manner.

"I will set a plate for you as soon as my legs cooperate." Saad rubbed his stiff knees.

James wrapped his arms around the rheumy-eyed slave and gave him a bear hug. "Take your plate and go sit in the garden or your room or wherever you like. I am too happy to eat."

"Maybe I should drink whatever you have indulged in," Saad said, shaking his head.

James erupted in a belly laugh. "I am sober as Apollo."

"How did the trial go?" Marcus asked.

"Horrible," James answered unable to stop smiling.

"Go for a walk to the market and get your fill of gossip." He dug a coin from his pocket. "Buy some honey-roasted nuts for Saad and you while you are there."

Sporting a grin wide enough to split his face, Marcus raced off.

Saad turned to Elizabeth. "A hard bump to the head, maybe?"

"Husband, pray tell us what has made you so... ah, happy." Libi wore a beautiful smile.

He circled the table, knelt before her, and clasped her hands.

"You, my love. You make me happy. I am choosing a life lived in the present and filled with joy and hope."

Her gaze shone as brightly as the sun. "If you say so."

How to explain the monumental shift? Words were cheap.

"I am going to spend the rest of my life proving I am a new man."

"No matter what, I will love you." She squeezed his hands.

"But you do not always like me."

Her lips quirked with a smile. "You have me there."

He grinned. "That will change, even if it kills me."

Her laughter was the sweetest of music.

Saad shuffled to the door as fast as he could move.

James hopped to his feet. "Stay, old friend. I have made a decision that will involve all of us."

The slave grasped the door frame for support. "Are you done with the lovey-dovey talk?"

James winked at Libi. "I will control myself, if you will?"

"We promise to be good." Her smile faded as she turned back at James. "What decision? Should I be worried?"

"You will be greatly pleased." He sat and covered her hand protectively. "I am repenting of my waywardness and will return to the priesthood."

Joy suffused her face. "Dear Husband, I rejoice a thousand times."

"You hated everything about being a priest," Saad said.

"I hid behind my hate. Abuses and corruption exist, but there are good priests and the Lord is good. All I can do is try to be a faithful servant."

"Nothing you could have said could make me happier." She kissed his cheek.

"You might change your mind when you hear this. I am setting aside my ambition to be a master builder."

"Have you told King Herod?" she asked cautiously.

"Not yet. He will not be happy, but that is his problem."

"Where do you plan to begin your search for your next patron?" More questions filled her eyes.

"Never," James replied with a smile. "That life is in the past."

She stared in shock. "Truly? But being a master builder was your dream."

Surprisingly, he did not have a single regret. "You and I are going to devote our lives to sheltering and caring for widows."

"I knew it," Saad mumbled. "He has lost his mind."

James shrugged. "I was hoping you would join us. But if you want your freedom, I will prepare the papers—"

"Where you go, I go," the old man said indignantly. "Who else would put up with your nonsense?"

"Perhaps Marcus will take my offer to free him." James knew he should not tease the man.

A worried look crossed Saad's face. "How is a one-armed boy supposed to make an honest living? I hope you will help me talk sense into him."

Saad was correct. Who else would have put up with his bitterness? Without these two slaves, he would have been totally alone.

"I will free you both and give you salaries. What do you say to that?"

Saad thought for a long moment. "If it makes you feel better. But it does not change anything. I go where you go."

"I have never received a finer compliment. Get going, old friend, before I come over there and kiss you."

Saad limped into the hall and his chuckles slowly grew fainter and fainter.

"Tell me more about this Jewish sect that aids widows," James said to Libi.

"You do not have to do this for me."

Her doubt was understandable. "Who says it is for you?"

"It is not your dream. It is mine."

"My dream is to tear down this nightmare of a house and replace it with a home for widows."

She laughed. "Your poor father would turn in his grave."

"A happy thought," James said in jest. "The truth is, I hate the idea of living here."

"Me too." She sighed. "It seems a waste to tear it down."

He pulled her onto his lap. "How about a compromise? We will remodel this monstrosity and build a smaller more modest home in a less crowded neighborhood."

She rested her head on his shoulder. "Are you sure this is what you want?"

"Would you have ever been truly happy living in

Herod's inner circle?"

"I would have tried."

"But what if you came to hate it and me?"

She nestled closer. "I love you. And nothing will change that."

"I want more than for you to tolerate our life." He stroked her back. "I want you to be proud of your husband. And to wake each morning eager to greet the day."

"Stop before you make me cry." She buried her face in his tunic.

"Wait until you hear it all."

She looked up. "Why do you sound leery?"

He took a deep breath. "I want to offer sacrifices at the Temple. You and I together."

She swallowed. "We can hope Jerusalem will be shocked speechless."

Libi's courage was always her finest trait.

CHAPTER 42

James stood with Herod atop the northwest tower of the imposing fortress guarding the Temple compound. Did the multitude of soldiers and priests manning the Hasmonean Baris find it ironic, as he did, that the day after Queen Mariamne was condemned to death on questionable evidence, the king would visit the fortress named for her heroic ancestors?

Herod leaned over the weather-worn parapet and pointed into the distance. "You cannot tell me you do not salivate over the thought of constructing a beautiful little theater overlooking the Kidron Valley."

A cold breeze whipped James's cloak. Dark clouds held the threat of freezing rain or a rare snowfall. The few people hurrying down the streets and alleys were those who had to be out.

"Nothing you can say will change my mind," James replied. "I have new ambitions."

"First Physician Hama deserts me and now you. Is it because of the queen? She left me no choice. You must see that."

James had been a young man when Herod fell in love with the graceful and lovely Mariamne, who had seemed equally taken with him. But over time Herod's unrelent-ing jealousy had soured the queen's love.

He was in no position to judge Herod. Under the guise of protecting Libi, he had forced marriage upon her. He could have sent her into hiding after rescuing her or en-trusted her to Gabriel's care, but consumed by his own selfish passions, he had taken what he wanted.

"My decision was made with my wife in mind," James said, wondering how he could have been so blind for so long.

"Elizabeth Onias never struck me as a delicate flower."

"I am not abandoning my vocation for fear of a peevish or disgruntled wife. Elizabeth is incredibly strong. She would never harp about the long hours of work required by a master builder or squawk over the need to move from workplace to workplace."

"That woman owns you." Herod snickered.

He had no wish to deny it. "Palace life does not suit us."

"Your wife detests sharing the same room with the man who executed her father," Herod stated benignly. "I cannot say I blame her."

All too aware the king's mood and attitude could change in an instant, James chose his next words care-fully. "She is incredibly forgiving and charitable. Her life had been a difficult one. I desire to make the rest of her days peaceful and happy."

Herod got a distant look in his eyes. "I almost envy you."

James was mightily tempted to suggest Herod exile his mother and sister and mother-in-law to a deserted isle.

"I am proof people can change. I am renouncing my apostate life."

"Are you?" Herod asked, intrigued. "Will you rejoin the

ranks of priests?"

"If they will have me."

"I will order High Priest Fabus to expedite the matter."

"With hopes of coaxing me into taking on the role of master builder to rebuild the Temple." James laughed grimly.

Herod clapped him on the back. "What makes you say that, my suspicious friend?"

The difficulties and dangers posed by Herod's tenacity could not be ignored. He would make it his mission to bend James to his will. The perfect solution presented itself.

"Elizabeth and I will not make our home in Israel."

"What? Where will you go?"

Regret stung his throat as he gazed at the city he had spent most of his life hating. Wasn't that typical of him, always swimming upstream? Only now he would not be alone. He laughed with real joy.

"I will give you an answer as soon as I discuss the matter with my wife."

CHAPTER 43

J ames raced home and found Elizabeth sitting with her cat on the porch outside their house. Her heart-shaped face was lifted to the sun. She was surrounded by several weed bouquets—gifts from Lydia and Kadar's children, who adored their aunt Libi.

He collapsed beside her and gasped for breath. "You grow more beautiful every day."

Libi laughed. "Age must be weakening your eyes, but happily it is working to my advantage."

Apollo woke from his nap on her lap and stood and stretched.

James patted the cat's head and was rewarded with loud purring. "Your hairy beast and I are making progress."

"Good boy," she said to Apollo. "I told you that you would like James if you just gave him a chance." She glanced up and her smile faded. "Did King Herod bite off your head when you gave him the news?"

"He was not pleased, but that is his problem."

"He could make life miserable." Her hand found his.

James grunted in agreement. "And if truth be told, you are probably worried I would eventually succumb to the pressure?"

"Maybe." Her tone remained kind. "Especially if he moves forward with his massive building projects."

He could picture the constant dust hanging over Jerusalem as Herod constructed amphitheaters, public bathing complexes, and a new grander palace. "He most certainly will transform the city and country. Of that I am sure."

Her eyes were full of sympathy. "It would be difficult for you to sit by and watch."

He had thought of that. "My blood flows with mortar and brick and chisel and hammer. Herod's does too, and he would use it against me at every turn. But I believe I have the perfect solution."

Apollo ambled away, allowing Libi to nestle closer.

"Do not keep me in suspense."

With his wife by his side, he felt as if he could conquer the world.

"At the risk of sounding like a hypocrite after accusing you of running away when you wanted to return to your work with widows in Egypt, I am going to suggest we do just that."

Her eyes widened. "You are in earnest?"

He drew her hand to his mouth and kissed her fingers.

"Hear me out before you agree."

A smile spread across her face. "What is there not to like?"

How could he not love his brave Libi?

"I would like to use our wealth to build and run homes for widows among diaspora communities, starting in Egypt, then maybe Greece, Rome, and Corinth. It would require a lot of travel and I hope you would work side by side with me."

"Yes, yes, yes. When do we start?" She practically glowed.

He would never grow tired of making her happy.

"Immediately, or I should say as soon as I make my triumphant return to the Temple." He groaned. "I have to work on my morose humor."

She patted his arm. "My grumpy puppy."

He made a face. "I knew your speaking to Kitra would not work to my benefit."

"I prefer it to Joyful James."

"You would."

They laughed like giddy children.

Libi sobered first. "What of your plans for rejoining the ranks of priests?"

He waved to Jachim as his elderly neighbor tottered outside, faithful to his daily routine of watching for the smoke of the Evening Sacrifice. "Thanks to my father, we are filthy rich and can return to Jerusalem as often as duty requires."

She rested her head on his shoulder. "What about your plans to transform your father's house into a home for widows?"

"I will leave the project in the hands of my stonecutter friends."

"You have thought of everything."

Her trust was a precious gift. "Saad presents a problem. It will take both of us insisting to force the stubborn man to take his ease while others wait on him and do the work of moving."

"He will hate that," Libi said, then sat up in excitement. "They are here."

James smiled at the sight of his oldest sister, her warrior husband, and their four children. "We will do well to be half as happy as Nathan and Alexandra."

Libi stood and waved. "I followed your sister around like a shadow, wanting her attention. And she was unfailingly sweet and patient."

The door to the house opened and Lydia flew down the steps, and she and Alexandra hugged and rejoiced over their reunion.

James watched in envy. He had been too selfish and self-centered a boy to give his sisters much thought. "It is time to learn if Alexandra is as forgiving as Lydia."

His sisters rushed toward him all smiles.

"Be ready to be kissed to death." Libi laughed.

He wrinkled his nose, but secretly welcomed the attention as his sisters showered him with kisses.

"Look how strong and commanding you have become," Alexandra said warmly.

Had it really been ten years since he had laid eyes on Lex? She was as bright and beautiful as he recalled. "It is good to see you, Sister."

"Come, Lydia," Alexandra spread her arms wider. "We are not too old for a sibling hug."

He and his sisters shared a marvelous crushing hug under the shadow of the bleak home that had held far too much misery. Bless the Lord, he and Alexandra and Lydia had all managed to break free of the pain and hate and find peace and love.

Old Jachim was watching, arms raised in joy.

James hoped to receive similar approval when he and Libi made their appearance in the Temple.

CHAPTER 44

The Temple gate loomed ahead. Elizabeth hesitated and cursed her churning stomach as Lydia and Kadar, accompanied by Alexandra and Nathan, smiled over their children's wide-eyed exclamations.

Eighteen years had elapsed since Libi had walked the hallowed Temple grounds. In her memories the courtyard surrounding the Temple had been a vast expanse of polished stones. But the gates, walls, the priest's precincts, and the Temple were all smaller than she'd expected.

She envied Lydia and Kadar their exhilaration and enthusiasm as they directed their youngsters to the money-changers' tables, where they would trade their Roman coins for Temple coins, before heading to the pens holding ritually pure animals and the booths for purchasing the appropriate grain offerings.

A large crowd milled near the Court of the Gentiles. Were they waiting to prevent her from entering the Woman's Court or to prevent James from proceeding to the Priest's Court?

Sympathy and love shone in James's eyes. His fast-growing black hair and beard had reached the shaggy stage in the week since forsaking his apostate ways. The scar marring his cheek would soon be swallowed up. Dressed in a humble brown robe, he had never looked more handsome.

"Kadar will bash anyone who attempts to stop us."

She glanced at the Levitt guards manning the Temple walls. Kadar and James had exchanged similar jests all morning. "I wish I could be as stoic."

"My bluster is all show." His smile faded. "You have displayed your courage over and over. You were a pillar of strength when captured by Judas the Zealot. You survived years of living as an outcast without turning bitter and hateful. You married Saul to save your brother Andrew."

"Still, I wish my mother and Gabriel and Leonidas could be here. I fear my mother may never feel well enough to travel to Jerusalem."

They were leaving for Galilee shortly to be reunited with her family.

"Are you dreading the prospect of spending time at my brother's olive farm?"

He chuckled grimly. "Only If Gabriel and Leonidas kill me for forcing you to marry me."

"Gabriel will understand." That was her dearest hope.

The bawl of a sacrificial bull pierced the air.

James hitched his thumb in the direction of the Temple. "First we have to survive today."

"I suppose we cannot put it off any longer."

"It is not too late to run for the hills." He winked.

A laugh bubbled up. "Life has never been easy or smooth for us. But that made us stronger." She raised her chin and walked ahead. "Today we claim our place in the

Lord's congregation."

James strode with her step for step.

"Before the roadside attack I could not wait to talk with my friends in the Men's Court when we should have been reciting prayers."

Some of her fondest girlhood memories were of holding her father's hand as they walked to and from the Temple. And sitting on her mother's lap in the Women's Court.

"The thing I missed most when I lived in Egypt was the rich scent of incense."

He wrinkled his nose. "It never quite covers the stench of blood."

Her feet slowed of their own accord as they approached the knot of people gathered beside the balustrade barring gentiles from proceeding any farther. She gathered her courage.

"My mother used to say—"

The crowd parted to reveal an older woman with silver-white hair.

Elizabeth flew to her mother and sought the comfort of her soft arms and warm bosom. "Mother! What are you doing here? The cold journey could not have—"

Wrinkled hands cupped her face. "Then I will die a happy woman. I just wish your father had lived. We prayed and prayed you would be healed."

Elizabeth covered her mother's frail hand. She had feared her mother would never recover after learning of Father's long-term affair with another woman.

"It is good to see you smile."

"How could I mope and stay sad with Gabriel and Shoshana spoiling me the way they do?"

Gabriel joined them. "Mother, are you going to share

Elizabeth with the rest of us?"

Her older brother was more muscular and his complexion a dark brown from years of tending to his large olive oil operation. It was difficult to believe he had once been a pampered Temple officer.

He had shocked the whole family when he joined the army to fight as a soldier in Herod's army. If that was not enough, he married a divorced Samaritan woman who had lived in a cave home. Gabriel was proof that destiny favored the brave.

"I am sorry we could not come sooner." He embraced Elizabeth and kissed her forehead.

Her heart swelled, and she hugged him tightly. She was no longer *zavah*. Her touch would not defile her priest brothers.

"Please tell me you will remain in Jerusalem for nice long visit."

Brotherly affection warmed his eyes. "Mother and Helen will riot if we do not stay for a week at the least."

"Sweet Helen." She released Gabriel and glanced around.

Her lovely sister-in-law Shoshana ushered forward an older girl and a curly headed boy.

"Helen does not like us to call her sweet," Gabriel said.

Helen was now a beautiful young woman. And seven-year-old Nehonya, who was named after their father, was the spit and image of Gabriel.

Elizabeth smiled through her tears—sad for all she had missed during her Egyptian exile, and at the same time overjoyed. "May I have hugs?"

Helen rushed to her, reserve giving way to sparkling vivacity. "Aunt Libi, you were always so kind and fun."

She had cared for her infant niece after Gabriel's first

wife died and came to love Helen as dearly as if she was her own child. "And you are lovelier and dearer than ever."

Little Nehonya hung back.

Shoshana touched her hand to his small shoulder. "This is your Aunt Elizabeth."

He ducked his curly head. "*Shalom*, Aunt Elizabeth."

"*Shalom*, my nephew. I hope you will call me Aunt Libi." She was instantly in love. Her nephew also represented hope. Shoshana had conceived later in life. Elizabeth prayed she and James would be blessed in the same manner.

Little Nehonya examined her with cautious eyes.

Gabriel had written faithfully over the years with stories and news about the children.

Elizabeth offered the boy a friendly smile. "Is it true you can knock an olive out of a treetop with a slingshot?"

"Father says he will get me a new slingshot if I do good watering and feeding our mules on this special visit to Jerusalem." He beamed with pride.

He could not be more adorable. "Will you teach me to use a slingshot?"

He giggled. "Helen was right. You are fun."

"I hope you will come and live in Galilee." Helen clasped her hand. "It is not so exciting as Jerusalem...but Father and Mother Shoshana plan to convince you that you will be happier there."

Elizabeth's breath caught. Did her brother plan to insist that James divorce her and that she go live with them? Is that why they had made the *special* trip to Jerusalem?

"The invitation includes your husband," Gabriel hurried to reassure her. He clapped James on the back. "*Sha-*

lom, Cousin, or I should say, Brother."

Gratitude and relief showed in James's glowing eyes and slow smile. "Your friendship and acceptance mean more than we can say."

"I am glad to see you are no longer so disagreeable," Gabriel said, and kissed him on both cheeks.

"I would not go that far," James replied, and directed a lop-sided grin at her. "I am sure I will still grumble too often and think uncharitably on others. But I will have someone to remind me of what is good and true and meaningful."

Life with James would not be a walk in an idyllic garden. Rather more like a sea journey visited with occasional rough waters and tempests, but also filled with gloriously sunny days and the reward of breathtaking sunrises and sunsets.

Her youngest brother Leonidas trotted up to them. He flashed a boyish smile. "Am I too late? I forgot I was wearing my sword. I had to ask a fellow soldier to hold it for me."

Gabriel rolled his eyes. "Leonidas has not changed a bit, as you can see."

Elizabeth tipped her head back. "You are taller and stronger, I can see that much."

Leonidas whooped for joy. He lifted her off the ground and twirled her in a circle. "Sister, how are you?"

She laughed and kissed his wind-burned cheek. "Wonderful now. I thought you were helping to guard the Nabatean border."

"My commander owed me a favor. And here I am."

"Put Libi down," Gabriel said, laughing with everyone else.

Nathan and Kadar's brood joined them at the same

time her brother Andrew approached, accompanied by High Priest Fabus and the other Temple officers.

Her heart sped up. Mother and the other women closed ranks around her. The men stood shoulder to shoulder in a show of unity.

Have pity on us, Lord. She prayed. *Have pity.* She met Andrew's eyes.

His face was not hostile. No, he was actually smiling.

She returned his smile.

What could be responsible for this change of heart? She did not know but rejoiced in it.

CHAPTER 45

J ames bristled. This was not the first time he had faced
down a High Priest of the Lord and the Temple officers. The difference was, he was not alone—his family and friends stood with him.

The support was both heartening and strange.

Ensuring Libi was not turned away from the Temple
was his chief goal. But how? Bribery and lies had worked
for his father. Whereas James had relied on insults and
rudeness. Neither were options today.

He lifted his hands to his robe in a familiar gesture.
Catching himself, he crossed his arms. "I come as a re-
pentant man." He waited for a rebuff, but none came. "I
seek purification for my wife and myself, so we may offer
sacrifices to the Lord."

High Priest Fabus stared back placidly. "As you should.
And what of your priestly duties?"

James had expected more resistance. Was this a trick?
He cleared his throat and continued. "I renounce my
apostate life and wish to return to the ranks of priests."

The High Priest nodded approvingly. "The Onias family is a noble line. Honor your name by doing good."

James had not been able to see past his father's evil to

see the good examples represented by his sisters and his cousins, Libi, Gabriel, and Leonidas. He made his promise to them. "From this day forward, I will strive to be worthy of the Onias name."

Gabriel stepped forward. "I can vouch for James's sincerity."

"Are you willing to undergo the prescribed punishments for your sins?" High Priest Fabus asked, then pointed to the chief treasurer. "And pay the large sums of taxes and tithes you owe?"

James hung his head, ashamed of his many offenses. "I will gladly submit to the deserved penalties and repay the required taxes and tithes."

High Priest Fabus nodded approvingly. "Andrew has asked to guide you through the necessary steps."

"Andrew?" James was thoroughly confused by the ease of the proceedings. "I will burn in hellfire before I divorce my wife."

Consternation showed on High Priest Fabus's face. "Nobody is asking that of you."

Which made James only more suspicious. He looked at his cousin for the first time. "I was sure you would have had something to say about our marriage."

Andrew's dour face held a surprisingly friendly smile. "Your neighbor Jachim came to the Sanhedrin on your behalf to clear up some important matters. The old man is quite fond of you. Just ask him."

Jachim approached, supported by his grandsons. A smile creased his ancient face.

"The council was interested to learn Simeon had confided in me about his...ah how to put this delicately... age-related deficiencies," Jachim said. "Thus his marriage to Elizabeth Onias was one in name only."

James's mouth fell open. His elderly neighbor had told the Sanhedrin his father was a shriveled up she-goat? More remarkable—they had believed the half-senile man.

"Simeon Onias treated you disgracefully," High Priest Fabus called over his shoulder, moving on, with the Temple officers in tow.

Old Jachim's eyes held a twinkle. "My wedding gift to you and your dear bride."

James continued to reel. "I can never thank you enough for your kindness."

"Come by when you visit Jerusalem and put up with a long-winded tale or two from your feeble-minded neighbor. That will be thanks enough."

James grinned. "It will be my pleasure."

"As a young boy you had a wonderful smile. It is good to see it once more."

"Libi and I are hosting a banquet this afternoon. You are welcome to join us."

"I have had enough excitement for one day." Jachim patted Banna's hand. "Take me home and you your brother can return and celebrate with your young friends."

The twin brothers departed with the promise to join them later.

Andrew had remained behind. "I am ashamed of my behavior." He bowed his head before James and his brothers and Nathan and Kadar.

James had been in Andrew's position too many times to judge. "You owe the apology to your sister."

Andrew turned to Elizabeth. "Can you forgive me?"

"Of course." Tears glistened in her eyes.

"Blessings on you, Sister." Andrew hugged her.

She hugged him back. "The Lord is good."

Her gaze met James's. "Shall we go and worship?"

James laughed with a joy far greater to any he had ever experienced. Constructing grand homes was something to boast over. But even the most magnificent of homes was still just bricks and mortar.

"'I was glad when they said unto me, let us go into the house of the Lord,'" he said, quoting from the Psalm of David, another tortured man.

CHAPTER 46

Following the blessing of offering sacrifices at the Temple, the entire extended Onias family, surrounded by a cloud of happiness, made their way out of Jerusalem and down the winding road to the Mount of Olives. Donkeys carried enough food and drink to feed an army.

Presented with the gift of a warm spring day, Elizabeth had suggested holding the celebration under the olive trees rather than in the gloomy house imbued with unpleasant memories of Simeon Onias. The others had readily agreed.

The spouting buds adorning the canopy of olive trees represented hope and new beginnings.

"Your smile has never been more beautiful." James helped her spread out a blanket.

The love in his eyes warmed her heart.

"This has been a favored spot ever since the night of the Maiden's Dance when your sister Alexandra and Nathan fell in love. The orchard aglow with candlelight and the white gowns were absolutely enchanting."

"Actually, my sister tripped, and Nathan caught her."

"Do not ruin my memories with the truth. As a thirteen-year-old girl, I dreamed of the day I would dance with the other maidens and capture the heart of a handsome young man."

"I wish I could turn back time and erase all the ugliness." He reached for her hand.

She threaded her fingers with his. "We will be happier than most because we will not take our love for granted."

The other women set out bowls of fruits and nuts and other delicacies. "This is our true wedding feast," she said contentedly. "Surrounded by family and friends. I will dream of this lovely day forever."

He kissed her cheek. "As will I."

Cheers and whistles came from the stonecutters gathered around the other men, who were giving swordplay lessons to the young boys armed with wooden swords.

James swiped his hand in a playful manner. "Go back to your warrior games, you barbarians."

"I'm glad you invited Pinhas and the other stonecutters," she said, smiling at the men. "They seem very likable."

"Only the angels know how I ended up with stonecutters as friends and warriors as brothers-in-laws. I stick out like a mule among stallions."

She squeezed his arm. "You are more like a war horse who runs his own way."

"I am going to view that as a compliment."

"Please do. And I will introduce you to all my unusual Egyptian friends."

"You sound as if we will spend our days on a leisure cruise of the Nile."

"Believe me, drifting on the Nile is boring...except for the crocodiles."

"After spending time with Cypros, Salome, Aalexis, and Phaedra, you know something about dealing with crocodiles."

"They are unhappy women." She brightened. "Did Kadar share the good news about Physician Hama and Kitra?"

"I did hear. But I did not think the middle of our wedding celebration was the best time to mention my ex-wife."

She laughed. "I am very happy for them."

Kadar and Lydia had offered to introduce Physician Hama and Kitra to their many friends and associates in Napoli. And they assured Avda he would soon have a thriving list of medical clients, starting with Kadar and Lydia's household. "I promised Lydia we would visit them very soon."

"You agreed quickly enough to Nathan and Gabriel's invitation," James said in a teasing tone. "We are going to be very busy."

Before leaving for Egypt they would spend a month between Nathan and Gabriel's olive farms. "Did I answer too quickly? Do you hate the notion of revisiting Galilee?"

"Because of this?" He thumbed the scar now hidden by his beard.

"I fear it will bring up unwanted memories."

"I was plagued more by shame than fear."

"You are the bravest man I know."

"Knowing you see me so is a precious gift, my dearest Libi."

They were victors indeed.

"Giving yourself permission to be happy is not as easy as it sounds, is it?"

His black eyes shone as brightly as a starlit sky. "No,

but we will spend the rest of our days making up for lost years. You will grow tired of hearing me say, 'I love you.'"

Was this much happiness possible? She cupped her ear. "What did you say?"

His smile was beautiful. "I love you."

HISTORICAL NOTE

Book four concludes The Herod Chronicles series glimpse into the early life of the man who is known to history as Herod the Great. By the time Herod makes his appearance in the New Testament gospels of Matthew and Luke he is nearly eighty-years-old and has been reigning as king of Israel for almost forty years. He dies in 4 BC, and his throne goes to his heirs, who are also identified as Herod in Biblical references. Thus the founder of the Herodian dynasty is referred to as Herod the Great and his sons and grandson as Herod Archelaus, Herod Antipas, and Herod Agrippa.

In the brief New Testament glimpse of Herod the Great, he meets with wise men from the East coming to him asking *Where is he who was born king of the Jews*? Threatened by the report, Herod calls for the execution of the region's two-year-old male children. A shocking response, wouldn't you say?

Why and how did Herod become the vicious, paranoid man we see in the Bible? This question was the spark behind the idea of the Herod Chronicles and using four heroes as mirrors of Herod's early years. Nathan and *The Warrior* show Herod as he makes his appearance in history as the promising but volatile Governor of Galilee. Kadar and *The Barbarian* depict Herod as an audacious and valiant fugitive and as a grieving son and brother.

Gabriel and *Warring Desires* depicts Herod as a successful and victorious military commander and merciless avenger. James and *The Apostate Priest* focuses on Herod as master builder, jealous husband, and distrustful king.

Herod was not all evil. By all accounts, he was a devoted son and brother. The economy prospered during his reign. He maintained peaceful relations with Rome. He was a talented and renowned master builder. He constructed what is known today as the Wailing Wall and the Temple Mount site of present day Haram esh-Sharif. He built the great port city and manmade harbor of Caesarea and reconstructed the stronghold of Masada and other fortresses into opulent palace fortresses. He was the force behind many dozens of other projects including pools and aqueducts, and to the outrage of many, a gymnasium, theater, and hippodrome on the outskirts of Jerusalem.

But, ruled by hatred and suspicion, Herod also emerges as an insanely jealous and distrustful man who executes the love of his life, Mariamne, and her mother, and eventually her two sons. His vengeance prompted the quote accredited to Caesar Augustus, "It is better to be Herod's pig than his son." The wasted potential is tragic. Herod the Great is a name that deservedly lives in infamy.

Two side notes should be pointed out. For the sake of the story, I changed Queen Mariamne's mother's name to Aalexis. Her name was Alexandra, but that name was already in use by our dear Lex. In our story I had the slave Niv deliver the love potion to Herod, but the actual culprit was an unnamed cupbearer.

There were historical High Priestly families named

Onias and Boethus, but James, Alexandra, Lydia, Phaedra, and Saul are fictional branches of those family and wholly my creation. Kitra and Taj and family are also a fictional family.

AUTHOR NOTE

Thank you for reading **Apostate Priest**! If you are so inclined, I'd love a review of Apostate Priest. Reviews can be hard to come by. You, the reader, have the power to make or break a book.

For more information about my books please visit my website: www.WandaAnnThomas.com

All the best,
Wanda Ann Thomas

WANDA ANN THOMAS' BOOKS

THE HEROD CHRONICLES

The Warrior (Book 1)
The Barbarian (Book 2)
Warring Desires (Book 3)
Apostate Priest (Book 4)

Inspirational Ancient World Romance

Faithful Daughter of Israel

BRIDES OF SWEET CREEK RANCH

(Sweet Historical Westerns)
The Mail-Order Bride Carries a Gun (Book 1)
Gunslingers Don't Die (Book 2)
The Cowboy Refuses to Lose (Book 3)
The Cattle Rustler and the Runaway Bride (Book 4)

ACKNOWLEDGEMENTS

Special thanks to my editor Susan Vaughan for her meticulous work. Timely and professional, Susan helped make the editing phase a stress-free and wonderful experience. I so appreciated Susan's encouragement and support with this project.

My beautiful cover was designed by Dar Albert of Wicked Smart Designs. The look and color- scheme of the Herod Chronicles series is simply lovely.

ABOUT THE AUTHOR

Wanda Ann Thomas is the author of Sweet Historical Western Romances and Ancient World Christian Romance. The common bond is my delight in LOVE stories. And creating stories is my happy place. After juggling a career as a dental hygienist and raising a family, I was ready for a new challenge. Twelve years and ten books later I am more enthralled with writing than ever.

Penning historical romances set among the tumultuous perils of the ancient world was inspired by my reading the works of the historian Josephus. The inspiration for THE HEROD CHRONICLES series came about while doing research for another project and learning the particulars of Herod the Great's career. A fascinating complicated man, Herod's larger-than-life exploits seemed made for fiction. Detailing the life and times of Herod also allowed me to explore my interest in the Roman world and my passion for heart-wrenching love stories, featuring warrior heroes and courageous heroines who will brave any danger for loved ones and struggle against overwhelming obstacles to win their happily ever after.

I'm blessed to be living my own happily ever after with my high school sweetheart turned husband. Our three beautiful children and their spouses and the grandchildren are the light of our lives. When not at my desk writing I enjoy playing a round of golf, or sitting by the pool, or watching my flower gardens bloom. Road trips are a favorite recreation. There nothing more I relish than the excitement of traveling to new places and touring museums and historic homes or exploring cities or visiting national parks. And refreshed and brimming with vivid sights, sounds, and images, I am just as eager to return home and plunge back into writing the next story.

—

Made in the USA
Las Vegas, NV
05 July 2022

51106081R00156